LETHAL BEAUTY & SMOKING STEEL BOOK TWO

MAFIAS
Embrace

DARCY RAY

COPYRIGHT

The unauthorized reproduction or distribution of a copyrighted work is illegal. Criminal copyright infringement, including infringement without monetary gain, is investigated by the FBI and is punishable by fines and federal imprisonment. Please purchase only authorized electronic editions and do not participate in, or encourage, the electronic piracy of copyrighted materials. You support of the authors rights is appreciated.

This Book is a work of fiction. Names, characters, places, brands, and incidents are the products of the author's imagination or are used fictitiously. Any resemblance to actual events, locales or persons, living or dead, is entirely coincidental.

Copyright @ 2019 Darcy Ray
Lethal Beauty & Smoking Steel: Mafias Embrace
First Publication: October 2019
Editing: Serious Moonlight Editing
Formatting By: Pretty In Ink Creations
Cover design by: Reaper Designs

All rights reserved. Except for use in any review, the reproduction or utilization of this work, in whole or in part, in any form by any electronic, mechanical, or other means now known or hereafter invented, is forbidden without the written permission of the publisher.

Publishing by Darcy Ray
AuthorDray@gmail.com

Dedication

Mr. D, you are my world. Thank you for supporting me in this crazy adventure and for being the eye candy for all my fans.
Nicole & Rowan, I love y'all. You guys are my besties and have been cheering me on the whole way.
My betas!!!! Each and everyone of you bitches are amazing and I'm super blessed to have such a great team like yall!
Ashley Lilly, thank you for inspiring me to write the MM scene. Its dedicated to you boo!
Finally, Chelsea, all dresses should have pockets and now all of Selene's and Octavia's do!

Trigger Warning

This is the only warning you will get. There is blood and violence in this book. Don't go getting pissy if you start reading this book and there is some kind of trigger for you. If you read Mafias Kiss, then you know shit is going down. I warned you on the first book and I'm warning you now - MURDER, BLOOD, SEX, CURSING, & DRUGS. That's what's in here. Oh, there is some MM in there. So yea, BE WARNED.

One

I STILL can't get over the fact that he is gone. It has only been three days since all hell broke loose, and I lost the only family I ever cared about. Looking around, I take in everyone standing around mourning, holding huge black umbrellas, and pretending they care. Unadulterated hatred runs in my veins; not one of these people has ever been there for him, never came to any major events at his club or even his birthday, and they have the nerve to pretend to care now. Hell, out of this crowd of hundreds, I can count on two hands how many people I actually know.

    A scowl slowly forms on my face thinking about how somewhere out there, his killer is still living. I would give anything to have him trade places—my father alive and the killer six feet under. But, no matter how much I wish or pray, I know he is gone.

His killer will be found. I will destroy him with my own hands and make him suffer all the pain Dominik went through, all the pain I went through, and hell, for all the pain my men went through. I will get revenge.

But for now, I will stand here surrounded by my men and listen to all the stories about the man I called father. I will let my tears fall freely, and I will say my final goodbye. Blinking back tears, I reach out and grab the closest hand I can find. Locking my fingers with his, I squeeze with all of my strength. It is taking everything I have to stop myself from breaking down and sobbing hysterically. Suddenly, the tremors I've been fighting hit me hard, and just as I start to collapse, the hand I am holding pulls me into a strong embrace.

Burying my face into his chest, I let my emotions loose, and start to sob uncontrollably. I tried to keep it in, I really did, but I just can't do it anymore. My tears mix with the rain and quickly soak into his black button-down shirt. Sobs rack my body and snot smears all over. I don't give two shits about looking like a mess, or the fact that I'm ugly crying. This sadness is weighing on me, so much so that everything around me is darkening.

The strong hands wrapped around me slide to my shoulders and shake me gently, but I refuse to look up. I just want to spill my tears against his warmth. Fingers dig into my chin, pulling me away from the dirtied material, forcing me to look up. The shadows still creep in from around me, covering everything with a black cloud. In the remaining light, I see him, the giver of my warmth, the strength to my weakness. Rain soaks Godfrey's inky-black hair, dripping down into my face, making me blink. With each blink of my eyes, my sight becomes clearer and clearer. Like, how his mouth is moving, but I can't hear the words.

Shaking away his grip, I try to bury my face again, but the bony fingers are back. Godfrey's grip is stronger this time, forcing my jaw apart. The blackness is nearly covering everything now, even Godfrey. The only thing remaining is his scowl while he is mouthing words to me. I still don't understand. None of it. Why did Dominik have to die? Why did Neal do it? What did I do wrong?

A sudden, intense, stinging pain shoots through my cheek, causing me to gasp, taking in the air I didn't know I was resisting. Palming my cheek, I take in more gasps of air, filling my lungs, allowing the oxygen to circulate through my body. Color overwhelms my senses, allowing the precise placement of pigmentation to fill in my surroundings. Taking a step back, I look around to see nothing but concerned faces.

A movement to my left causes me to spin on my heels—Joe, my Russian god. Taking slow steps, he makes his way over to me. Fire is still scorching my cheek underneath my palm, and a slow but steady throb is growing. A gust of wind blows through the crowd causing my drenched hair to wrap around my face. Pawing at the wild turquoise strands, I finally get them unstuck and flip them over my shoulder. Joe finally stops in front of me. Reaching out, he gently grabs my wrist and pulls it away from my face, allowing the salty rain to streak down the inflamed skin.

The murmurs that I keep trying to ignore only get louder. Single words make it through my protective wall of men. Disaster. Failure. Overthrow. Whore. Each one feels like another slap to the face. Even though metaphorical, they hurt worse than Godfrey's hand ever will. Seeing my distress, Frank loudly claps his hands together, making everyone jump. His booming voice startles them once more. "The funeral is over. Say your final goodbyes and leave." The fake-ass people only stand around for a second. Some look as if they want to argue, but the murderous look on Frank's face dissuades them.

It takes nearly an hour for the crowd to disperse. Each person stops in front of Dominik's grave, either laying a rose on top, saying a quick prayer, or even just standing there in silence. With each passing person, I regain control of myself, and the pain on my cheek starts to disappear. As the numbers dwindle to fewer than twenty, I spot a familiar face.

I only take a few steps toward her before I catch her attention. But as soon as I do, her unshed tears fall. Hurrying over to her, I wrap her in one of the best hugs I can manage. My sobs quickly begin to match hers, and all the emotions I just gained control over break loose. Doris starts to mumble into my chest, but I can't understand her through the sobbing. Instead of asking her to repeat herself, I wrap myself tighter around her and slowly rock side to side.

I haven't seen her since the last time we went to the diner. Even with that, I still think of her as family. Resting my head on her crown of silvery black hair, I whisper, "Thank you for coming, Ms. Doris. I didn't realize how close you were with Dom." My statement nearly crosses the line of a question, but I know this isn't the place nor time to discuss such matters. However, it lets her know the window is there when she is ready to talk.

Nodding her head, she gives me one last squeeze and releases me. Her mascara is running down her cheeks, and her subtle lipstick is smeared. Turning toward Jaime, I motion for him to come forward. With a simple nod of his head, he makes his way over. Stepping up to my side, he reaches into his jacket pocket and pulls out a pack of tissues. Holding them out to me, he says, "*Mi amor*, tissues?"

Reaching out, I grab the pack, pull some out, and hand them over to Doris. "Here, you have some . . ."

I trail off, not sure what to tell her, but she catches on and nods her head in understanding. Taking the tissues from me, she starts to wipe her face as best as she can. With the square material in front of her face covering the mess, she lets out an embarrassed laugh and says, "Silly me, I should get going. Um . . . stop by the diner sometime; I'm sure there are things you want to discuss."

"Of course, Ms. Doris, make sure to drive safely." Nodding her head, she looks once more toward the casket and then turns to leave. Instead of watching to make sure she makes it to her car, I keep my eyes locked on the man who I loved as a father. Blood-red roses frame his motionless body as it lays in the pure-white silk-lined wooden box. Diamonds encrusted into the matte black wood shimmer under the scattered rays of sunshine, and thanks to the moisture that is still lingering in the air, rainbows shine in various directions.

The sight in front of me is beyond beautiful, and with the gloomy mood weighing down on everyone, it is a much-needed distraction. As the last person takes their leave, I make my way over, and with every step, I take a breath.

In.

Out.

Left foot.

Right foot.

Reaching my hand out, I run my fingers through the vibrant colors that dye the air. The warmth of the sun that is breaking through the clouds lasts only for a few seconds as I continue down the path toward him. Leaves crunch behind me making me aware that I am not alone for this. Even with this knowledge, my hands still tremble. Grasping them in front of me, I take the last couple of steps and stop with only a couple of inches separating us.

He is too pale. His silver beard no longer looks full or alive, his cheeks are sunken, and his chest no longer rises. Shit, nor is mine. Dragging in a shaky breath, I reach my hand toward his. A chill shoots through me as I come into contact with him. Grasping his bony fingers, I lower my head and let out a quiet prayer. I don't know who I'm supposed to pray to, or if they even exist, but as the words slip past my lips, a small weight lifts off my shoulders.

Amen.

Looking around me, I notice Viktor, Joe, and Godfrey surrounding me. Each one of them with puffy eyes and various reddening on their faces. I'm not the only one who lost someone, no, they lost their uncle. Biological or not, he cared for them. My eyes linger on Viktor and watch as all of the little movements he makes causes him to wince in pain; 'Scratch,' my ass. During the gunfight, he got a gnarly slash on his abdomen that required a long line of stitches. Reaching out to him, I grab his hand and give it a squeeze. Joe moves to my right and wraps his arm around my waist, allowing me to lay my head on his shoulder.

Godfrey takes the spot behind me and grasps both my hips, pulling me against him. Their connection is what I need. None of it is sexual in any way; it's meant to ground me here, so I don't let the darkness overtake me again.

I'm not sure how long we stand like that, but the sound of someone clearing their throat drags us back to reality. Looking over to the other side of the coffin stands the groundskeeper. Clearing his throat once again, he says, "Ma'am, I have to lower him down now. It's about to storm again, and well, I respect Mr. Romanov too much." My eyes skim over his dark, leathered skin and his frail physique. How he will manage to shovel all the dirt on top of Dom's casket goes beyond my knowledge. His dirt-covered jeans are tattered and worn, his red, flannel button-up shirt looks like it's seen better days, and his shoes, well, I can see his curled pinky toe nearly poking through.

As I reach his eyes, I notice the jaundice-like color overtaking them. Tilting my head to the side, I let my curiosity get the better of me and question him. "How do you know Dominik?"

"Ma'am, I've been the groundskeeper here since I was sixteen. I've buried many people in my days, a lot of them with the family ties back to Mr. Romanov. Usually, people ignore me or scowl at me for burying their loved ones, but not him. He made it known that what I was doing is important and precious. After the fourth time we met, I noticed he started coming up here nearly every day. Always to the same spot, making sure to brush away the leaves or replace the flowers. But then his visits became fewer and eventually stopped altogether. With how good he has treated me, I made sure to take extra care of that spot. Sure enough, almost a year later, Mr. Romanov came back to bury another." I watched him make his way over and noticed the shock on his face as he saw the new flowers I placed earlier that day.

"Long story short, he was grateful for my care and started giving me an extra stipend to make sure it stayed cared for. But I didn't need the money, so instead of pocketing it, I use it to make sure everyone has fresh flowers and hired others to help care for the people buried here. "

Pulling another tissue out, I dab the tears that are streaming down my cheeks. Dominik always found beauty in death; he was never scared of it and always embraced it. Taking one last look at my father, I nod my head for the groundskeeper to start his process.

Reaching forward, he gently closes the coffin lid, making sure it doesn't slam, and then removes the faux grass that hides the six-foot drop. The sounds of the lift lowering Dom become too much for me to handle. Taking a few steps back, I shake my head, and I yell out to whoever is listening. "I can't watch this; I need to go." Turning on my heel, I stumble past Godfrey and practically run toward our waiting limo.

My heels sink into the damp earth, causing me to lose one on the way, but I don't stop. Instead, I kick off the other and run the rest of the way. I can barely see where I'm going through the tears clouding my vision. I stumble over small headstones and just as I reach the edge of the field, my toes catch on a flat one, sending me flying. Luckily, I land on soft green grass, but that doesn't soften the blow of my pain. Curling into myself, I wrap my arms around my knees and let my tears spill onto the earth.

A few seconds later, I'm lifted off the ground. Opening my eyes enough to see who it is, I am shocked by who I see. Wrapping my arms around David so he won't drop me, I let him carry me the rest of the way. Stopping by the door, he lowers me down to my feet and holds onto my shoulders to steady me. I somehow manage to get to the door open and crawl inside.

Before he can close the door, I motion for him to wait. "Thank you, asshole." Even though he scoffs at my comment, I notice a small smile form. He doesn't say anything to me in response; instead, he closes the door and turns to stand guard. Crawling over to the long bench, I lay on my side and silently wait for the others to join me.

It's nearly an hour later before the door opens again. The sky outside is dark from the storm, and the wind is blowing the trees around, almost like a hurricane is upon us. I watch as everyone climbs in and takes a seat wherever they can. Before the interior light can turn off, I notice the dirt covering Vik's, Godfrey's, and Joe's slacks.

Seeing my confusion, Frank answers my unspoken question, "They each buried him. It is the greatest honor they could have. Putting Dominik to his final rest."

I stop myself from crying again. I need to be strong for my guys. They all look as if they are barely holding it together—even Jaime looks rough. Making sure my eyes connect with all of theirs, I give them all the words they need to focus on. "We will avenge him. Neal was the one who pulled the trigger, and he nearly killed me. He will pay. Everyone who betrayed us will pay."

Two

IT'S BEEN four days since Dominik was laid to rest, three hours since my last visit with Tavia, who is still in a coma, and ten minutes since the last call from Dom's lawyer. He has been pestering us about reviewing the will and testament, and I know we should get it over with, but doing that will only make this final. I don't want anything else to change. I can't handle it.

My phone vibrates on the counter next to where my head is laying. Barely lifting my head, I glance at who it is. "Ugh, does he not quit?"

Frank's thick hands stop massaging my back so he can grab my phone. Swiping open the message, he quickly types a short text and then slides the phone onto the counter. Then, he startles me by clapping his hands loudly, nearly making me jump off the bar stool. "Alright princess, you have two options. You get up, shower, and go to the meeting I just set up or I make you shower and go."

Sitting up from my depressed perch, I cross my arms over my chest and scowl at him. "Fuck, Frank, when did you become my dad?"

Shaking his head, he quickly grabs me by my waist and throws me over this shoulder. His grip is so tight I can barely wiggle around to get out of his hold. His chest rumbles as if he is talking, but I don't catch anything he is saying, "You talking shit mean-ass?! Speak louder so I can actually hear you!" He doesn't retort back; instead, he marches us to my bathroom, where he slides me to the ground.

With brisk movements, he undresses me, leaving me mixed with shock and annoyance. I'm standing butt-ass naked when he finally speaks again. "You ARE taking a shower. You stink. It's been what? Three days. They may coddle you and let you mope, but I'm not dealing with it. You are putting on your big-girl panties and washing that fine ass of yours."

Well, shit, who am I to argue. Lifting my arm, I take a sniff of my armpit and instantly regret it. I pull back quickly, and my eyes catch my reflection in the mirror. I can't help but gape at the atrocious monster staring back at me. Stepping closer, I get a better look at how far I let myself go. My normally thick and wavy turquoise locks are flattened down by the weight of the natural oil, my skin is overly shiny, and sure enough, there is something stuck in between my teeth. Letting out a sigh of defeat, I turn toward Frank and say, "Alright, you win. I'll shower and clean myself up. What time do we have to be there?"

With his thick arms crossed, he nods his

head in approval and starts to leave. Before he walks out of the bathroom door, he turns back to me and says, "I told him we'd be there in two hours. That will give you and the guys time to shower and get ready. Now I'm going to go over there to get them moving. Oh and I sent Jaime home, he needs to catch up at work and caring for you is only pushing him further behind."

Reaching over, I turn the shower to depths-of-hell hot and wait for it to warm up. Looking back toward Frank, I catch his gaze roaming over my naked body. For the first time in weeks, I feel the need to be ravished flowing through me. Letting out a laugh, I walk over to Frank and give him a quick kiss. "Go and round them up. I'm too dirty at the moment for you to get me riled up. As for Jaime, well we will have to discuss that matter later."

After a quick slap to my ass, he leaves my apartment and heads next door to the apartment that houses four of my five guys. Steam fills the walk-in shower and is now rolling out onto the floor. No longer procrastinating, I walk in and clean all the grime from the last couple of days off me.

By the time I emerge from my bathroom, I feel like a whole new person. My breath is fresh, my hair is back to its bouncy self, and my skin is flawless once again. With the meeting being semi-formal, I decide to wear a black high-waist skirt, a white long sleeve shirt with a deep V-neck, and my classic black stilettos. Even with my energy nearly depleted, I still force myself to apply a few simple applications of makeup. Grabbing my phone, wallet, and keys, I make my way next door.

Even though I have my own home, I basically live here with the guys. Before Dominik's death, I would alternate which guy's room I slept in each night. So when I walk through their door without knocking, no one is surprised. However, their glances toward me let me know they are pleased to see me up and moving. By the look of things, Frank achieved his goal to get everyone ready because they all have damp hair, and they are in various states of dressing.

Looking around their apartment, I notice they have let it go. Pizza boxes and cans litter any flat surface you can think of, dirty clothes are piled up high in the hall, and dirty dishes are stacked high in the sink. I'm not sure what is worse, a dirty home or a dirty body. I guess everyone handles their sadness differently. Where they trashed their home, I deep-cleaned mine, so much so that I had to open my windows to vent the bleach smell out.

"Right, when we get back, I'll clean the apartment. I don't want to hear any arguments." They chose to be smart and keep their lips sealed shut. Instead of arguing, they quickly get dressed and finish just as Frank walks through the front door.

Looking at us, he nods in approval and then heads back toward the door. Swinging it open, he turns to glare at us. "Alright, I got the car pulled up front ready to go. I won't be going because I have matters to attend to at the club, also well, this is a family-only kind of thing."

Godfrey is the first to make his way toward

the door, as he passes by me, he grabs my hand and pulls me with him. Joe and Viktor trail behind us, and as I pass Frank, I get on my tiptoes and kiss him goodbye. "I love you, Frankiepoo."

"I love you too, princess, now go, we all got shit to do."

Tugging my hand, Godfrey propels me down the hallway. We crowd the elevator and stand together in silence as it makes its way down. No one wants to talk about what is to come or the fact that we all have slacked way too hard for the past two weeks. People are counting on us, and we have been holed up doing nothing but eating, sleeping, crying, and pigging out. As the elevator door dings open on the main floor, we spill out and walk to the valet stand. The receptionists greet us like they are supposed to, but as soon as they assume we are out of range, they start to gossip. About what? I honestly don't care.

In the middle of the entrance sits a white SUV. Fuck, why can't we stick with the usual black? White is too fucking bright for how I'm feeling right now. I know the guys agree with me because I hear a chorus of grunts and groans. Moving forward, I climb into the middle row, allowing Viktor to claim the front passenger, Joe in the seat next to me, and Godfrey in the third row.

Ever since the funeral, I've made sure David is part of our entourage, so he is now our designated driver. We may have a hateful relationship, but he has proven his loyalty and support since I've become the boss. David was completely devastated to learn that his partner was the one who killed Dominik. Hell, he denied it for three days straight, until he saw the video surveillance that caught the whole thing. By the way he is gripping the wheel, I still don't think he is over it one hundred percent.

"David." My voice is nearly a whisper, but with how quiet we are being, I know he hears me.

Releasing his hands, he whips around and looks at me with a confused face. "Huh? Oh, um, sorry. I was already informed of where to go. We will arrive in approximately twenty-three minutes."

Giving my most sincere smile, I say, "Thank you for that, but David, if you need more time to cope or whatever, all you have to do is let me know."

"No offense ma'am, but sitting at home won't change things. I have new responsibilities, a new mission, and a new boss. So please, just let it go."

I've never had such a civil conversation with him before, so listening to all his pleasantries leaves me in a semi-shocked state. Not wanting to cause any issues, I drop the conversation and fasten my seat belt. The guys are all lost in their phones responding to business emails, so I turn my attention outside and watch the buildings fly by. My mind wanders, and as we pass the homeless shelter, I think back to nine years ago. I would probably be dead if it wasn't for Dominik. Looking down to my phone, I realize what day it is. In two weeks, it will be ten years since I stumbled onto the drug deal gone bad, since I played an evil version of Russian roulette, and since I realized I actually wanted to live.

Joe's fingers gently swipe the tear that escaped its prison, which makes me look away from the rundown buildings. Turning my attention to Viktor, who has his AirPods in his ears, bopping to whatever is playing, Godfrey is on his MacBook, and Joe is looking at me with such a loving expression. I'm not sure what made them walk into my life or what cosmic forces are to blame, but I will be forever grateful. They have been keeping me afloat during my darkest times, even though they have been suffering just as much.

"I love you. All three of you. I haven't told y'all, and I know this isn't the perfect time or place, but I fucking love y'all." My little speech is as much of a surprise to me as it is to them. As my words sink in, they turn their attention toward me. Seconds go by, and no one says anything, so out of nervousness, I start to sputter nonsense. "I'm sorry, I know it's too soon, and you guys don't have to say it back. I just don't want to go another day without letting y'all know how I feel."

Pulling an earbud out, Vik slowly turns his head toward me and whispers, "Say that again."

Slowly turning in my seat so that I am facing him completely, I repeat what I said, but with fear of rejection laced in my every word. "I love you guys. Not platonically as friends, but I legit love each and every one of you."

"You're lucky this vehicle is moving or else I would have you in my arms right now, doll. Fuck, I love you too, babe, with all my heart."

Viktor's words come out like he is choking back tears, so I lean forward and place my hands on his shoulders. Reaching back, he grabs hold of them and turns his head enough to give them each a soft kiss.

Godfrey's careful fingers trace my spine over the flowing fabric of my cotton shirt, leaving goosebumps in their wake. Following the trail from his fingers, he starts to place delicate kisses in the same path. I stay completely still, except for my chest rising from the shallow breaths I keep reminding myself to take as his breath tickles my neck. I shiver with anticipation as he reaches the sensitive spot on the back of my ear.

Shooting his tongue out, Godfrey lets it flick over the spot for a second before moving up to my earlobe, giving it a quick nip that is hard enough to draw blood. No matter how much I want to reach up and grab my ear, I know that doing so would only displease Godfrey, so instead, I dig my nails into the thickly corded muscles on Vik's shoulders. Letting a slow breath slip past my lips, I turn my head to the side to see him out of my peripheral vision. The smirk on his face is nothing but scandalous. As if he knows the pain he caused was more pleasurable than painful.

"Blue, never doubt our love for you. Like I told you all those months ago, you ensnared us the moment Dominik sent us a picture of you. He only wanted to show us the little girl who dared to stand against the never-losing cold steel and won, but he started something that day. The fire we saw in your eyes through the photo was raging, and it still is. *Góa ài lì*, I love you." Each and every word that came from Godfrey's mouth is nothing but pure silk that slides its way into my ears and wraps around my heart, giving it a little squeeze. My dark assassin may be the quietest of the bunch, but when he does speak, it's beyond reproach.

Feeling the love that is coming from my beautiful men, I start to feel overwhelmed with more emotions, but this time, instead of woeful feelings dragging me down, joyous butterflies lift me up. A tear streaks down my cheek, but before it falls, Joe reaches over and catches it with his finger. Releasing Vik's shoulders, I lean back in my seat and turn, so I'm facing them all.

Moisture starts to collect on my lashes, so I quickly wipe it away and let out a forced laugh. "Gah, sorry. I've been super emotional with all that's been going on."

"Princess, you don't have to apologize, you lost one of the most important people in your life, and now you are surrounded by three men who love you to the moon and back. We would never think less of you for showing how you feel. God knows how much we love you." Warmth spreads across my cheeks, letting them see just how much their words affect me.

A cough from the driver's seat makes us turn our attention toward David, who glances at us through the rearview mirror. Glancing back to the road, he says, "We are less than a mile away from the lawyer's office. There are tissues in the back of Viktor's seat, so fix your runny makeup before you make us all look bad." Comfort washes through me at the familiarity of the sarcastic words that usually pass between us. However, this time, I keep my crazy, bitchy attitude in check and focus on cleaning up.

Reaching my hand into the little pouch in the back of Viktor's seat, I dig around for the little pack of tissues. In the process, I bump across a couple of different tubes in varying shapes and sizes. Out of curiosity, I pull them out to see the exact same brand of eyeliner and mascara I usually wear. Unable to hold in my snarkiness, I continue to dig around and call out to David. "Awe look, asshole fucking pays attention." Peeking through my lashes, I see him scowl in annoyance that only triggers my gut-busting laughter which causes the others to join in.

The feeling of the SUV being put into park makes us all quiet down and look out the dark-tinted windows to the ominous black brick building that holds the man that is going to make everything final. I let out a shuddering breath at the thought. Turning my focus back to fixing up my face, I quickly reapply my makeup to make myself presentable again. When everything is put away, I place my hand on the door handle and mumble to myself, "Well, I guess it's now or never."

Three

A CHIME sounds as Joe pulls open the heavy wooden door which allows the rays of sunshine to flow into the dimly lit office. With the gust of fresh air pushing its way in, a tidal wave of dust and smoke rolls out. I don't think I can arch my brow any higher than it is now, but with how dingy this place is, I wonder if it's all a scam. Looking back toward David, I ask, "You sure this is it?"

Pulling out his phone, he taps on it for a few seconds and then glances at the crooked cast iron numbers above the door. Nodding his head, he replies, "Yeah. That's it." Well, okay, then.

Sighing, I make my way in. In order to see, I have to squint my eyes and nearly close them. To the left is the dark wood receptionist desk with an empty chair. A small lamp on the corner of the desk flickers as if it's hanging on for dear life. Manilla folders and papers cover the entire surface of the desk, except for the small space where a steaming styrofoam cup sits precariously close to the edge. Scanning the rest of the room, I see old-fashioned couches that look as if they popped out of a seventies furniture magazine lining the wall with a coffee table dead center. Multiple ashtrays overflowing with butts and ashes are placed randomly around the sitting area. Well, I guess I know why it's so smoky.

Taking a few steps forward, I approach the desk, rap my knuckles loudly, and call out, "Hello? Is anyone here? I have an appointment." I decide to keep what my reasoning for being there vague, just in case it really is a set up. The less they know, the better. The sound of someone hacking up a lung nearby lets me know that we aren't alone. Still on high alert from everything that has happened, I motion for the guys to investigate.

Viktor takes the lead with his Glock pulled out and starts his way down the hall. Following right behind him, Godfrey steps into the darker areas of the hall and hides in the black abyss. After a few moments, they are beyond what I can see, so I turn toward Joe, who is still holding the door open to let in as much light as possible. Pushing some papers aside, I slide myself onto the desk and patiently wait for my guys to return.

It only takes a few more minutes before three bodies emerge from the dark abyss of hell. The man that is being pushed out into the open has his hands raised in surrender and looks exactly how I imagined him—wearing only a stained wifebeater and threadbare jeans.

Topping it all off is a lit cigarette bobbing between his lips and shitkickers covered in what I hope is mud. Godfrey and Vik don't remove their guns from the back of his head until he is standing in front of me.

His eyes dart around in a skittish way, assessing us to see if we pose a threat. The moment his gaze lands on me, he instantly realizes who I am. With stuttering words, he quickly tries to apologize for his absence, but before he can even get a complete sentence out, I give him the hand, making him pause. "Look, I'm not in the mood to deal with any blabbering, nor do I want to be here. But to my dismay, it's pertinent that I speak to the lawyer who will be reading my father's will." My voice is laced with anger. Couldn't we wait another week?

Shooting his hand out, I notice how tremors are overtaking it. Sweat slicks his palm, and his nails are stained yellow, probably from long-term smoking. I don't hesitate to reach out and grab his hand. But this shake is not going to be pleasant. Instead of a gentle shake, I squeeze with all the strength I can muster and force his knuckles to grind together. His face morphs into a grimace and then to distress as he tries to pull away but can't. His jaundiced complexion washes out to an almost ash-white shade, and he quickly apologizes. "I'm sorry ma'am, I didn't hear anyone come in . . ."

"Psh, that's because you are two sheets to the wind." Viktor's outburst makes me arch a brow, glancing from Vik to the guy whom I suppose is the lawyer.

Clearing his throat, the man continues, "Like

I was saying, I didn't hear anyone come in, and business has been slow. My only client just passed, and when his family kept avoiding my calls, I assumed all was done."

Releasing his hand, I wipe the sweat on my skirt and slide off the desk. Ignoring the sputtering man, I make my way to the hall. As I pass Godfrey, I run my hand over his and drag him along with me. Stepping next to me, he wraps his arm around my waist and slides a few fingers into the top of my skirt. His fingers are rough from handling his weapons, but lean and nimble at the same time, so as they work their way down, little shivers erupt all over my skin. Looking up to him, I see his darkened expression, but he doesn't look my way. Instead, he faces forward and leads me down the dark hall, which leads us to a room full of empty desks.

From the sound of shuffling feet, I can tell that they followed us, so without looking back, I call out, "Which office?" Out of nowhere, a deft hand slides its way up my back, down my arm, and threads itself with my fingers. I don't even worry about who it can be; no one is dumb enough to fuck with me with my men so close.

"Excuse me, pardon me. Follow me this way, ma'am, and um . . . sirs." Squeezing past the three of us, the squirrely man heads to the right which has a line of doors. Nodding my head, we follow behind him and into the room he opened the door for. Inside the room, there is a large oval table with six chairs surrounding it. In the center sits a crystal vase stocked full of wilted roses. Tears threaten to spill once again, but after a few quick breaths, I have my mask back in place.

Breaking loose from my guys, I walk around the table and claim the head chair. As soon as I'm seated, everyone else takes their spots. Joe and Godfrey take the chairs on either side of me, and Viktor sits next to Joe. Standing at the other side of the table, the lawyer grips his chair and rocks back and forth on his heels. Rolling my eyes at his nervousness, I turn my focus back on the roses that are in Dominik's signature vase. Out of curiosity, I ask, "When is the last time they were replaced?"

He looks confused for a second, but as soon as he sees where my attention is, his face softens, and he responds. "They were sent over just over a week ago. I . . . I just can't change them out." I have the same issue. The roses that were on my island were beyond dead. They had started to rot in the vase. Until one day I went into the kitchen and they were gone. I don't tell him that, no, that thought I keep to myself.

I'm not sure how long the room sits in silence, but the sound of Viktor slamming his hands on the mahogany table startles everyone out of the trance we were in. Clearing his throat, Vik says, "Let's get this reading over with, I'm starving."

The lawyer jumps into action; he lets go of the chair and scurries out of the room. Loud thumping and a string of curses follow after him, and only a few minutes later, he returns with a safe deposit box and a thick manilla envelope. Sitting down in the chair, he lays everything out in front of him and looks to all of us. "These types of things are usually recorded for security reasons, but Mr. Romanov is—I mean was—a very loyal customer. I know there are things that are better left unsaid, so I will withhold recording. Now to start, everything in this safe deposit box is to be given to a Ms. Doris Nettles. The instructions are for me to tell a Ms. Selene to hand-deliver these personally to Ms. Doris."

Nodding my head, I wave for him to continue.

"With that out of the way, I'll continue to the property Mr. Dominik Romanov owned. The first property on the list . . ." I zone out as soon as he starts. All I can hear is blah blah blah and bits and pieces of words every now and then. The only thing I can focus on is wondering what's in the box for Ms. Doris. What is Dom's connection to her?

I am almost completely zoned out when the sound of my name brings me back. Looking up from the table, I see everyone staring at me as if they are waiting for some kind of reply. I don't even hide the fact I wasn't listening. Instead, I stand from the table and walk over to the lawyer with my hand out and say, "Where do I sign? I'm over it. I don't want to be here. I'll read through all the fine print later." Looking down on him, I finally notice his name tag. "Doyle. So that's your name." With nothing further to say, I snatch the pen from his trembling fingers and hastily sign the several pages that require signatures.

With the last signature done, I toss the pen down and walk out of the office. Tracing my steps back toward the front, I surge through the hall with the need to escape this dark and depressing place. I don't pause for the people calling my name behind me. Instead, I yank the door open, making it nearly fly back and hit me. As soon as the fresh air hits me, I take in a deep, cleansing breath and hold it in for as long as possible. Just as the black spots start to form, I slowly exhale all the bullshit that I've had to deal with in the past couple weeks.

As the next breath of air fills my lungs, a new resolve starts to form. I can't be as soft and carefree anymore. I'm the goddamn mafia boss! There can't be any more tears, no more breakdowns, and for fuck's sake, no more people dying! Taking the feeling of straight badassness, I bottle it up and store for when it's needed. I don't need to be a fucking savage when it's only my men and me. No, I can let my guard down when they're around. They won't judge me for being the big ball of emotions that I am.

Surveying my surroundings, I spot the SUV we arrived in and walk toward it. Sliding in, I ignore David's probing gaze and buckle up. Shrugging his shoulders, he turns the volume up on the radio and waits for the others. It only takes them a few minutes to wrap up their conversation with Doyle before joining us in the SUV. Once they are all in their seats, David looks at me through the rearview mirror and says, "Where to boss?"

Pulling out my phone, I check the time, and sure enough, we are still within visiting hours. With my eyes locked on his, I respond, "Take me to see Octavia, I need to check on her." With a nod, he breaks eye contact, backs out of the parking lot, and merges into the increasingly dense traffic. Thankfully, the hospital is only two miles away, so we arrive in no time. David drops us off at the back of the hospital so we can avoid curious eyes and access to the elevator that leads directly to Tavia's floor easily.

As we all pile into the metal box, I shoot Frank a quick message letting him know where we are, and within a few seconds, he responds.

F: Don't forget our dinner date tonight, princess.

S: I would never do such a thing, I need some us time.

F: Anything for my princess. Spend time with ya girl. ILY.

As the elevator opens, I walk out smiling after reading his last message. I know he verbally tells me that he loves me nearly every day, but reading it is different. As we walk down the sterile white hallways of the hospital, my smile begins to fade. Beeps from the machines in each room, single words from the nurses as they talk, and the soft whimpers from the patients fill my ears. As I pass the nurse's station, I stop in front of the charge nurse to get a quick update. "Any news on Octavia?"

Without glancing away from her computer, she shakes her head no. Gah, I just want to grab her by the back of her head and slam her face into her screen. The silent treatment she is giving me is uncalled-for and is definitely not appreciated. I understand she is working, but twenty seconds of her time will not kill her, though ignoring me might. I've put up with her bullshit for the last two visits, and I'll be damned if she thinks this shit will fly. Turning away from her, I run through all the possible things I can do to her in my mind.

Crossing the last couple of feet to Tavia's room, I feel my heart lift with the hope that she is awake. Rounding the door to her room, I look over to the bed. Letting out a breath, the hope I carried walking in simmers down to nearly nothing. It's been nearly four weeks since she fell into a coma, and with each tick of the clock, the chance of her waking up gets lower and lower. I'm the person she assigned to make all decisions in these types of situations, so turning off the machines is up to me. I'm not ready for that. I can't.

Walking over to her limp form, I grab her hand and give it a squeeze to let her know I'm here. The only response I get is the steady beeping of the machines that show the life inside of her. Godfrey, Viktor, and Joe claim their seats while they wait for me to finish my visit. For the next forty minutes, I talk to my best friend and clean her up to the best of my abilities. When we leave her room, she has freshly painted nails, brushed hair, shaved legs, and of course, her signature red lipstick. She will wake up, and when she does, I want her to feel as normal as possible.

Four

AFTER LEAVING the hospital, we made our way over to the Sub Rosa. As much as I want to hide out in my apartment, Frank had a point. It's time to press play and stop leaving life on pause. So here I am, sitting in Dominik's old office, spinning in slow circles in his—my—office chair. I'm supposed to be reading and organizing the files to get familiar with everything, but going through them feels like such a violation. Pulling out my phone, I hook it up to the surround sound speakers and blast my playlist. Giving myself one final spin, I close my eyes and decide to tackle whatever my gaze lands on.

As I spin, my equilibrium becomes off balance and makes me sway unsteadily in the chair. After a few seconds, I finally come to a stop. Slamming my fist down, I quickly squeeze my eyes closed and then slowly open them. "Huh, I guess I might as well get it over with." Dominik's intimidating desk stares back at me with its multiple drawers probably chock-full of documents and vital information pertaining to the mafia and all of its important business transactions. Scooting forward, I start at the top and work my way down.

Pulling open the center drawer first, I'm relieved to see mundane office supplies such as pens, highlighters, markers, Wite-Out, and staples. It only takes a few minutes to organize things and throw out the used sticky notes containing nothing but random scribbles. Satisfied with my progress, I open the next drawer, and this time I'm not so lucky. From front to back, there is nothing but vertical file organizers stuffed with papers. Pulling the first one out, I start to read, and instantly something catches my attention. In bold, red lettering is *Assassinations: Past and Future*. Mumbling to myself, "Well shit, let's not start off easy. Just dive right in." Shaking my head, I start to read everything, word for word. The more knowledge I have, the more powerful I will become.

Nearly four hours later, I'm finally finished with the last drawer. Thank god Dom was organized and labeled everything or else this would have been a whole lot worse. Just as I kick the drawer to close it, the wooden base shifts. Leaning down, I carefully lift the board to reveal a false bottom. What the fuck. Laying in scattered piles are newspaper clippings, documents, and a single photo. Picking up the picture, I suck in a breath. The little girl in the picture could have been me, well, that is if I were born a decade earlier. Her light blonde hair shines in the sunlight, her genuine smile shows pure happiness and love, and she is surrounded by nothing but vibrant red roses. The similarity to Dominik's signature roses is uncanny. Before I can dive any deeper into the hidden compartment, hands slide onto my shoulders.

Whirling around, I start to swing on whoever fucking dares to touch me. Thankfully, I realize who it is before my knuckles connect with his face. Laughing, I pause the music and turn to face Jaime. "You're lucky I didn't knock you on your ass, *papi*!"

His muscled chest shakes with laughter. Taking a step back, he throws his arms up in mock defense. "Woah, watch out, we got a badass in here." Jaime's smart ass comment is filled with lightheartedness and is exactly what I need after looking through these intense files.

Forgetting about the picture in my hand, it falls into the drawer as I rise from my chair. My knees pop in protest from being seated so long, and I groan with each pop. By the time I'm fully straightened, Jaime's amused expression only becomes more jovial. Reaching over, I smack him and jokingly say, "How dare you laugh at my old age! I'm thoroughly appalled!" I try to play up the act, but the look on his face makes me start laughing hysterically and soon enough he joins in.

Jaime's lighthearted personality is definitely something I need. I can't remember the last time I laughed so hard in the past three weeks. As our laughter settles down, it feels like a million pounds have been lifted off my shoulders. Closing my eyes, I let myself bask in the feeling of happiness. In the midst of it all, Jaime's

Spanish accent spills over my thoughts in rich caramel tones. "*Mi amor, te pareces a un angel.* Light shines around you like a halo, your dimples show just enough to make you look beyond beautiful, and your laughter is like the purest gift from God himself." Each of his words caress me in a way I never thought imaginable.

With hooded eyes, he takes slow and steady steps toward me. As he advances toward me, I step backward until I am backed against the desk. With hunger in his eyes, Jaime continues to creep even closer until his body becomes flush with mine. With each heaving breath I take, my chest rubs against his, causing my nipples to become alive and pert. Warmth spreads from my chest up to my cheeks and down my body until it reaches my now throbbing core.

Leaning forward, Jaime starts trailing soft kisses from one side of my neck to the other. Bracing my arms on the desk, I relax my head back, allowing him to explore even further. As he reaches the bottom of my ear, he starts to make his way to the spot behind my ear that he knows drives me crazy. With a gentle blow to my hotspot, I let out a low moan and flutter my eyes until they close from pleasure. The next thing I know, his strong hands latch onto my hips with a punishing grip that I'm sure will bruise. The combination of rough and soft and sensual is something I've been craving.

Overwhelmed with desire, I tilt my pelvis and press even closer to him. Jaime pressing back against me is the only thing I need to know that he is turned on as much as me. His rock-solid dick strains against his jeans, and with each movement of my hips, it twitches and moves right where I need it. To still me, he tightens his grip on my hips, causing his nails to bite into my skin through my shirt. Before I can protest, he places me on the edge of my desk and swiftly wipes it clear, causing everything to crash to the ground.

Letting out a growl, I say, "You're lucky I want you because I think you just broke my laptop." With fumbling fingers, I start to undo his jeans. With the button undone, I quickly yank the zipper down and slide my hand inside to find the prize. Much to my surprise, Jaime went commando today, so there isn't another barrier preventing me from clasping his silken cock and stroking it. As my fingers reach the head, I let my finger run over the slit, and the feeling of pre-cum greets me. With a swipe of my thumb, I gather it up and bring it to my mouth. Locking my eyes on his, I dart my tongue out and relish the taste of his essence.

His eyes dilate as they focus on my full lips encasing my thumb. In the next second, he is tugging his jeans down and pushing my skirt up over my hips. Gripping my thighs, he tugs me to the edge, my ass nearly dangling off the desk. Leaning over me, Jaime pushes the deep V of my shirt to the side and exposes the luscious curve of my breast. My nipple is already at attention from all the raging hormones flowing through me, but as soon as the blast of cool air flows over it, it tightens even more. Damn near hard enough to cut glass.

Stepping forward, he slides his hips in between my thighs and presses himself against my lace-covered pussy. Leaning down, he latches onto my nipple and lavishes it, alternating between sucking and biting the sensitive areas around it. Pushing the other side of my shirt over, he switches sides and begins to lavish my other nipple as well. All the while, he is grinding himself against my throbbing pussy, making it weep my sweet nectar as it begs to be filled. Reaching up, I grip his hair and push him lower. With a pop, he releases my overly sensitive nipple and obeys my silent command.

As he slowly trails kisses down my stomach, he reaches up and hooks his thumbs into the thin material separating us and starts to tug it down. By the time he reaches my throbbing core, I am completely exposed. Dropping down to his knees, he tosses my legs over his shoulders and doesn't hesitate to dip his tongue inside my pussy and feast on my juices. Jaime's tongue works me over like a sensual lover, caressing and showing every inch the passion it deserves. I throw my head back and release a string of curses the second he latches onto my throbbing nub.

It doesn't take long for my legs to start shaking as my impending orgasm creeps closer and closer. Not able to continue supporting myself on shaky arms, I lay back and lose myself in the sensations flowing through me. Sure enough, the ball of pleasure building inside me reaches the edge, and all I need is a few more seconds of pleasure before will explode. But just as I start to spasm, Jaime stops his assault on my pussy and keeps me from going over the edge.

Releasing a frustrated groan, I start to lean

up and yell at him for stopping, but before I can even move, he stands up. With my legs still on his shoulders, he grabs his cock and rubs it up and down my slit, coating it with my juices. With each swipe, the head of his dick nudges my clit, keeping me right on the edge but never pushing me over. Getting frustrated, I try to take matters into my own hands, but before I can do anything, he slams into me, forcing a cry of pleasure out.

Not pausing to allow me to adjust to his girth, he continues to pump into me with deep, hard thrusts. Throwing my hands back, I grip the edge of the desk to keep myself from sliding off. With each thrust, the desk shakes, and so do my legs. Without warning, I finally crash. A scream is ripped from me, but he doesn't relent, if anything he fucks me even harder — each thrust punishing and unforgiving. I get no time to come down from my euphoric high; instead, he keeps me in a blissed-out state which has my channel gripping him like a vice, and the tremors keep rocking through me.

Looking at him, I watch as he looks down at our connection with a face of pure satisfaction — almost like a kid in a candy store. Sweat starts to collect and run down his body. A droplet catches my eye as it trails past his chest and down his tightened six-pack abs. Right before I can watch it slide down his pelvis, Jaime tilts, which causes him to slide against that sensitive spot deep inside me.

Letting go of the desk, I grasp my breast and start to pinch and swirl my straining nipples. With each powerful thrust, I slide back until my head hangs over the back of the desk and when I open my eyes, they land on Frank who is leaning against the wall with his hooded eyes locked on the connection between Jaime and me. My eyes trail down his body and stop at the bulge pressing against his faded jeans. Tearing my eyes away, I focus back on Jaime, who looks like he hasn't even noticed our audience.

I just started to come down from euphoria, but between the sound of Jaime slamming into my gushing pussy and the pure thrill of knowing Frank is right there watching, I quickly climb again. The moans that escape me mix with the groans coming from Jaime, but at the sound of a grunt that comes from Frank, Jaime freezes. His eyes dart from Frank to me and back again. Indecision laces his features, so to help him, I drop my legs off his shoulders, wrap them around his hips, and nudge him to continue.

To my dismay, he doesn't get the hint, so I lean up on my elbows and glare at him. "You better keep fucking me or else I'm going to have Frank finish me off." Nearly thirty seconds pass, and he hasn't made a move, so I look at Frank and wave him over to me. When Frank takes his first step forward, Jaime grips my hips and flips me on the desk so that my ass is in the air.

A deep throaty laugh erupts from Frank which makes me drag my eyes up his authoritative form. Standing only a few inches closer with his arms crossed over his chest, he lifts his chin and with a gravelly voice, he says, "You sure you know what you're doing? My princess likes it rough, and her pussy is fucking greedy. If you wanna tap out, now would be the chance."

Scoffing at Frank's comment, Jaime's smooth hand glides over the curve of my ass and up my back. Once he reaches my shoulders, he pushes them down. I can hear Jaime's response through the sound of my heart pounding in my ears. "No worries, old man, I can handle her. I don't want you breaking a hip." Their egos are battling each other, and the testosterone permeating the air has me trying to squeeze my thighs together as my core starts to ooze more of my nectar.

Jaime kicks my feet apart, which spreads my legs wide, and then he grabs my wrist to pin them behind my back. The only warning I get to brace for him is pressure from the tip of his dick lining up with my entrance. This time, he slides in slowly but doesn't stop until he is fully seated inside me. The position he has me in is keeping me from moving around, and my thick turquoise waves are blocking my view. Growing frustrated with his lack of movement, I swivel my hips in hopes of achieving some much-needed friction to get me back on the edge of euphoria.

In response to my movement, Jaime lets out a grunt and finally start to fuck me. With every thrust, he picks up speed until he is finally back to his punishing pace, which turns my moans into whimpers, and they quickly become screams of pleasure. Through my messy hair, I can see Frank walking over until he stops right in front of me.

With his thick, calloused fingers, he moves the hair of my face and runs his hand down my face until he gets to my jaw. With a steady grip, he lifts my head until I can no longer arch my neck, and what I see in front of me instantly makes my mouth water. Bobbing not even an inch from my face is Frank's rigid shaft, so with a flick of my tongue, I guide it into my waiting mouth. Frank's hand curls into my locks, allowing him to grip a handful, and he starts to fuck my mouth without restraint. The dual penetration overwhelms my senses and makes the tight ball of pleasure grow bigger and bigger. I'm almost to the verge of exploding, but I just can't get enough.

Jaime must be sensing the battle I'm fighting, because I feel something wet land on my puckering rosebud, followed by one of his digits. The feeling of all three of my holes filled suddenly becomes too much, and I explode. White spots flash across my vision and tremors pulse through my pussy that is milking Jaime, who stills and grunts as he spills his seed inside me. Frank follows right after and lets out a bellow as his cum spills down my throat. I make sure to swallow every last drop as he starts to pull out of my mouth.

Frank relaxes his grip on my hair and allows me to lay my head down on the cool desk to catch my breath. Jaime lets go of my wrists, staying rooted deep inside of me before he collapses on top of me. The thudding of his heart beats through his chest, and together we take deep calming breaths. In front of me, Frank tucks himself away, steps to the side, and picks something off the ground. The next thing I know, there is a tissue in my face. With gentle hands, he wipes away the mess that comes from giving head — the tears and snot.

After a few minutes, Jaime finally lifts himself off me and pulls out, leaving me empty and full all at the same time. With a grunt, he motions to the tissues and says, "You mind handing me that? I need to clean our girl up." There's no point in even arguing with him. My body is too exhausted to want to move, let alone clean up the juices that are leaking from me. After some shuffling, Jaime quickly cleans me up with the same amount of gentleness that Frank had, and helps me off the desk. My legs are shaky, and my hair is a mess, but damn, I feel fucking amazing. Letting out a sigh of relief, I straighten my skirt and fix my shirt.

Looking around my office, I see all my desk items scattered around on the floor. With a wave of my hand, I motion to Jaime and say, "Don't forget to clean up your mess. I spent hours getting this damn desk organized." With the desk in the forefront of my mind again, my eyes glance down to the bottom drawer. Squatting down, I remove the items in the hidden compartment and close the drawer, making sure to lock it in the process. Straightening up, I grab my phone and keys and start to make my way out of the room.

Just as I open the door to my office, Jaime says, "That's it? You're just going to leave?"

With my back to him, I give him a shrug and say, "What did you expect Jaime? Cuddling and whispering sweet nothings?" Turning to face him, I see confusion and hurt etched on his face. "Look, I got shit I have to handle, and you have to get ready for work. I'll text you later, mkay?" Pursing his lips, he nods his head and quickly starts to collect his clothing to get dressed. Shaking my head, I turn to the door and walk out, leaving Frank and Jaime behind.

Five

IT'S BEEN two weeks since my rendezvous with Jaime and Frank in my office. Since then, I haven't heard a single thing from Jaime. From reports that Frank is giving me, Jaime is still alive and kicking—going from work to home, and that's it. I honestly don't have the time nor patience to deal with pouting. Ever since I became boss, my schedule has been jam-packed. On top of all that, I'm considered the weakling. I have no experience doing this whatsoever, so I need to prove my place and learn whatever I can as fast as I can.

Thankfully, all of Dominik's documents have been very informative and have served as my study guide. It's like he set it up that way on purpose. As for the papers that were in the hidden compartment in the bottom drawer? They sit in my purse, burning a hole, begging to be looked at. I know that they have a deeper meaning than I can handle at the moment, so I keep them tucked away, out of sight, and out of my mind. Those kind of distractions are not something I need right now, not when I'm meeting the import dealer and a handful of the prostitutes that work for me.

Viktor, Joe, Godfrey, Frank, and I are all piled into Godfrey's burgundy Range Rover as we make our way over to a warehouse about thirty miles out of town. I've never been to this warehouse, but this is a regular place for Vik, so we let him drive. With his wounds fully healed and all the stitches out, he can start resuming his normal shit. I don't know who is more excited out of the five of us. Viktor because I'm allowing him to work again, or us, because we don't have to listen to his bitching about being stuck on the couch.

I don't care how overprotective I was being. He was injured, and the doctor ordered him to stay off his feet. Even with the all clear, I'm still making him take it easy. The thought of possibly losing someone else turns my veins into ice. Fear flows through the frozen channels and shoots directly to my heart. Fighting back the urge to grab my chest, I ball my hands into fists and squeeze. The gentle purr from the engine mixed with the humming from one of the guys slowly calms me. The conversation they are having is a simple reminder that they are there. I don't catch what they are saying, but from the bits and pieces I do catch, it's a light topic.

For the rest of the ride, we all sit in peaceful silence, completely absorbed in our phones, catching up on the encrypted messages and text messages. Times like these seem to happen more and more. With every day that goes by, I get less time to spend with my guys, less time to myself, and no time to breathe.

I'm not sure how much time has passed since the last word was spoken, but it's been long enough that I startle when Joe speaks, jump a little in my seat. Licking my lips to moisten them, I turn toward him and confess to being distracted. "What was that? I honestly wasn't paying attention." I try to clear my throat, but it's thick from being too dry. Reaching down, I take a quick swig of water, but as I finish, a rogue droplet slides down my chin. Before I can wipe it away, Joe leans forward and gently caresses his finger over my chin, collecting the droplet.

My eyes track his hand as he slowly brings it up to his parted lips. With a flick of his tongue, he collects it. The ice inside of me instantly thaws from the pure, raw masculinity sitting so close to me. The heat starts to spread and heads straight to my core, which makes it throb with desire. Pulling my gaze from his mouth, I trail up his strong features until I reach his waiting blue eyes. Knowledge of the effect he has on me shines in his deep blues.

Laughing, he repeats what he said. "We should be arriving in twenty minutes or so. I sent a mass message to all the bitches and told them to show up. Also, I got word that there is a group of girls wanting to get worked in."

The fire inside me dims at the thought of those girls wanting to become ladies of the night. I bet most of them will be younger than twenty-five, and some of the others will probably be just over seventeen. Recalling what it was like for me when I was in their position, I know I have to change things to ensure they don't have to deal with the same shit I did—the cold nights, the hollow emptiness of hunger, and the excessive thirst from not having clean water in days. I may be the boss of a notorious crime organization, but that doesn't mean the people who work for me have to suffer. Well, until they fuck me over. Then they will wish they stayed in the infested building that they came from.

As their employer, I need to make sure they are in optimal health to earn me the most amount of money. That not only includes their physical health but their mental health as well. Taking another quick swig of water, I twist the cap back into place and turn my attention back to Joe, who is texting up a storm. I nudge his knee to get his attention, and with a grunt, he responds, "What's up sweets?"

"Do we have a doctor for these girls, and when was their last screening for diseases?" More questions build up behind my lips, but Joe holds out a hand to stop me before I can voice them.

With a glint of humor in his eyes, he waves me off, and says, "I got it all covered. Everyone gets screened every thirty days, condoms and birth control are mandatory, and psych evaluations are every three months. Dominik owned an apartment building just on the edge of town, and that's where they stay." Knowing that he has everything under control removes some stress that I didn't realize I was carrying around.

With one thing off my mind, I turn in my seat so that I can face Viktor. His eyes are trained on the road, but as we drive over a bump in the road, I notice a grimace flash across his face. I know asking about it won't lead anywhere, so instead, I focus on the deal that lays ahead. From the information Vik gave me earlier in the week, the dealer we're meeting with is one of our best importers. The drugs are one hundred percent pure, and the guns are unmarked and made with the strongest quality metal. For as much as we pay, I expect nothing less.

Not much later, we pull up to a privacy fence that stands at least ten feet tall with no way to peek inside. On the driver side of the SUV, there is a keypad and intercom system. Leaning out the window, Viktor enters the code and presses a button which I assume buzzes the security room. Immediately a harsh yet familiar voice sounds through the intercom. "Who the fuck is it?!"

A haggard cough gets cut off as he lets go of the intercom button and I can't help but smile. It's been nearly ten years, and I still remember the voice that grumbled through the phone when I made my life-changing call. Out of the corner of his eye, Viktor sees the smirk on my face and raises an eyebrow at me. Without taking his eyes off me, he pushes the button again and says, "Ay old man, it's Viktor. I got the boss with me." The crackling static of the intercom is the only response we get, but right after it ends, the mammoth gates slide open, revealing a large compound.

As we drive in, I take in the heavy security guarding the area—two at the entrance, two at the door of the compound, four walking in intervals around the fence line, and two in towers on either side of the property. They don't fuck around here. Viktor doesn't stop driving until we pull up to the massive compound. After a few ticks, a sliding door starts to roll up, exposing the inner workings of the facility. Everything is open and exposed except for an area partitioned off into a sizable room. On the outside of the room, there are rows of shelves that nearly reach to the second floor. Every shelf is lined with wooden crates, each varying in size.

We finally come to a stop near the stairs that lead up to the second floor. Lost in taking in my surroundings, I don't realize that my door is open. Godfrey's smooth hand glides over my cheek, startling me. With an embarrassed grin, I slide out and join the rest of the guys near the bottom of the steps. No one says anything as we ascend the stairs. The only sound is the loud clacking of my shoes against the grate and the beeping from the forklift roaming around the shelves.

As we reach the top of the stairs, we come upon a large sitting area and scattered around are all the ladies and the men that work for me in the prostitution ring. Dominik took pride in the pussy that worked for him. None of them have STDs, none of them are hooked on drugs, and they all have a place to call home. I wasn't much different than them not too long ago. The only difference was my job title made it legal. Politicians didn't need to know I was fucking my clientele, that was my fucking business. Hell, I've even had a politician a time or two.

With a welcoming smile, I wave to them and

say, "Thank you for being here on such short notice. Your respect is noted and appreciated. Today is going to be a long day, so when it's time for you to meet with me, don't fuck around. There is still going to be a nightly quota to meet." Without waiting for the onslaught of questions, I walk past the door that Vikor is holding open for me.

On the other side, Joe stands with a bemused look on his face. As soon as the door is closed, he says, "Laying the law early, I see." Humor and appreciation pour from him, letting me know I haven't fucked up yet. Draping his arm over my shoulder, he starts to lead me down a short hallway. Bumping into my hip, I look up and see his shining blues staring down at me and with a smirk he says, "I know you're all new to this shit, but do what you think is best. If anything is questionable, one of us will let you know."

God, the warm and fuzzies are real with him. Lifting up on my tiptoes, I plant a quick yet passionate kiss on his waiting lips. As we separate, I smile up to him and confess, "I love you, babe. I'm probably going to make fucked-up decisions here and there because I am nowhere near perfect. But knowing I have y'all at my side to help me is more than I can hope for."

"Honestly, you only had a crash course training and Dominik's notes to go by. There haven't been any threats from the other gangs on the outskirts, and the income is still steadily increasing. Just focus on what you think is best, and the rest will work itself out." Moving up beside me, he pulls out his phone and shows me a picture. "As for now, you have a meeting with this guy. His name is Sasha, and he's our main importer for weapons, their accessories, and some of the narcs that we distribute."

The man in the picture is not who I expected to see today. Instead of a brute, Sasha is prim and proper in a tailored business suit. Before I can assess his details any further, Joe leads us into a large meeting room where a glass-and-black-steel desk takes up most of the space. In the center of the sleek desk is a crystal decanter with some kind of amber liquor and a crystal vase holding a bouquet of Dominik's signature roses. A pang shoots through my heart, but this time I hide it. I can't let his death continue to tear me down. I must remain strong and prove I was meant to be the boss.

Stepping up to the table, I run my nails on the glass and walk around to the front where my chair awaits. Instead of sitting, I observe the office and watch Viktor, Frank, and Joe walk to a nearly black window. Continuing my walk, I make my way around the table to join them. As I get closer, the details on the other side become clearer, and I realize we are looking at the area where our vehicle is parked. But instead of just our SUV, there is another one parked beside it. Men in black suits stand near the back passenger door, and from their movement, I can tell they are speaking into mics.

Speaking to anyone in general, I say, "I'm guessing that's Sasha?" As soon as the words leave my lips, the man himself steps out of his vehicle and straightens his suit. "Well, I guess that answers my question." As if he can hear me, he turns his gaze up to the window. His gaze is so intense that goosebumps erupt over my skin. Yanking my eyes away, I turn to Viktor and say, "He can't see through this, right?"

Shaking his head, Vik turns from the window and walks up to me. Placing both of his hands on my shoulders, he says, "No doll, he can't." Planting a quick kiss on my forehead, he walks around the table and says, "I'm going to escort him up, make yourself comfortable."

Walking back to my chair, I plop down and look between Joe and Godfrey, who are both moving to take their seats. "Anything I need to know about this guy?"

With a grunt, Godfrey is the first to respond. "He doesn't know that you are the new boss. He is a playboy at heart but loyal to the bone. Sasha has worked for Dominik for over ten years and not once has the quality of his product been less than superb."

A scowl transforms Godfrey's face into the dangerous assassin I know him as. Not understanding the shift in his attitude, I ask, "So why do you hate him?" He starts to shake his head in denial, but I stop him. "Don't lie to me. It's all over your face."

"He hates him because Sasha has asked Dominik for your hand in marriage several times. Dominik denied each request, but Sasha was still persistent in his quest to marry you." Joe's blunt statement leaves me shocked and a little appalled.

I don't get a chance to respond because Viktor chooses that moment to open the door and usher Sasha and his crew into the room.

Hanging in the grasp of the last two guards is a large suitcase which they carefully lay at the opposite end of the desk from where I'm sitting. While everyone gets situated and seated, brief flashbacks of the massacre flash through my mind. Anxiety rockets through me and my heart starts to beat rapidly. My nails rhythmically tap on the table, and my leg starts to erratically bounce as I try to release some of the anxiety flowing through me.

With a clink, Godfrey slides a tumbler of liquor in front of me. Without much thought, I toss the drink back, slam it on the desk, and motion for him to give me a refill. The burn of the warm amber liquid running down my throat distracts me from my current situation and allows me to relax even further. With a fresh drink in hand, I sip it slowly and enjoy the flavors.

I'm not sure how much time passes, but the sound of someone clearing their throat pulls me from my anxiety and alcohol stupor. With finesse, as if I just didn't have a mini panic attack, I wave my hand, and say, "Please proceed, I'm ready to get this over with."

A rich laugh slips past Sasha's full lips even though it looks as if he is trying to hold it together. Unable to control himself, he erupts in a full belly laugh that is so contagious most of the whole room follows. Not me, though. Instead, I take in the guards and then my eyes finally land on the man of the hour. With a fully-groomed beard and a slick comb-over fade, he looks like a perfect mix of rugged and wealthy. The only indications of his age are the crinkles that surround his soft-blue eyes and the silver that reflects the light scattered throughout his hair and beard.

Though he must be nearing his late forties, he exudes confidence and sexuality as if it's second nature. Sensual and dangerous, a deadly combination. A hum of approval vibrates my lips that are resting on the rim of my drink, and as I continue to eye fuck him, he glances my way. He holds my gaze and dares me to look away, challenging me on who's the boss here. Smirking at him, I play his little game.

No one sees this exchange, and as every second ticks by, my grin grows wider and wider. Arching one of my perfectly-manicured brows at him, I wait for him to give. With a tick in his jaw, he nods his head slightly and looks away. Satisfaction spreads through me and to celebrate my little victory, I down the rest of my drink in one last shot. *That's right, bitch; pussy always wins over dicks.*

Six

WITH TWO drinks down and another one being poured into my cup, I can quickly envision this meeting turning into chaos. My filter crumbles from the dark liquor, and so do my boundaries. Taking what I want, even if I know that it's going to burn. Something about Sasha draws me in, almost like a moth to a flame. His hypnotizingly blue eyes have swirls of gold that are as mesmerizing as the flickering dance caused by fire. The sheer thought of all the naughty things he could do to me causes me to heat up, in more places than one.

Leaning back in my chair, I bask in their camaraderie and let their lighthearted mood wash over me. I know we are supposed to be here for business, but seeing genuine smiles on the faces of each of my men is worth the wait. Scanning my eyes over them, I catch Frank's intense gaze. Awareness radiates from him, which tells me all I need to know. He saw how I checked Sasha out, how I squirmed in my seat, and probably even saw the flush that flared across my cheeks.

Giving him a subtle nod and a playful wink, I let him know there's nothing to worry about. Even though Sasha causes a warm kindling inside me, it doesn't compare to the inferno my men cause. Accepting my response, Frank leans back in his chair and lazily crosses his arms. Patient and demanding all at the same time. Sighing, I raise my tumbler and loudly clear my throat. With that, their attention turns toward me and their voices quiet.

Silence greets me, and with that, I start the meeting. "Sasha, thank you for coming on such short notice, it's greatly appreciated. Since your last visit, shit has changed." Pausing, I watch as his brows bunch, and he lifts his hand to stroke his trimmed beard. "As you know, Dominik Romanov was recently murdered. What you don't know is that night, he appointed me his underboss. As you know, that—"

"*Podozhdite minutu.*" Jumping up from his chair, he starts to pace the floor, and on his third lap, he turns his attention back to me. Arching a brow, I patiently wait for him to continue. Shaking his head, he sits back down and props his elbows on the table."Are you telling me that *you*, my blue-haired pixie, are the new boss?"

Nearly choking, I can't help but laugh at his remark. Shaking my head, I reply, "Well geez, if you say it like that, it does sound kinda crazy!" Standing up, I casually walk over to Joe and reach for the knife I know he stashes in his pocket. As I reach down to grab it, I give Joe a brisk kiss on the cheek. With my back facing Sasha, I straighten and wipe all emotion from my face. I can feel the curious glances from my men, but they don't act nor question what I'm doing.

In one swift motion, I have the knife open and pressed against Sasha's pulsating jugular. His guards react, and with fumbling motions, they draw their guns and aim at me. Pressing the blade even harder into his sun-kissed skin, I watch as a droplet of blood escapes its protective barrier. As the blood trails down his neck, he slowly raises his hand and waves off his entourage. None of my men are even fazed by their animosity; they know what I'm doing, and they watch the game play out right before them.

Leaning down to his ear, I whisper, "Let's get one thing straight, I'm not your girl. I never will be, nor do I wish to be." Before I pull the blade away, I slide it up his neck until it's directly under his chin. Turning his head toward me, I press my slightly-parted lips to his and give in to the curiosity that has been clawing at the back of my mind. Curiosity will not kill this cat.

The moment our lips touch, Sasha braves the steel digging into the underside of his jaw and pushes his way inside. His tongue caresses the inside of my mouth with a demanding force, drawing mine out. Pressing the tip of the blade deeper into him, I lean back and nip his bottom lip hard enough to get a hint of iron on my tastebuds.

Pulling away from him, I watch as the blade that is pressed into him separates from his skin. Surprisingly, he is only left with a red mark despite his movement and the force I was applying. Closing the blade, I slide it on the table to Joe and return to stand in front of my seat. Noting the guard who now looks dumbfounded, I continue where I left off. "Like I was saying, I'm the new boss, and all business will run through me. From everything I heard about you, and from the stories my men have told me, you were fiercely loyal to Dom. I only hope you will be the same way with me. Now, let's get this business meeting over with. What did you bring me today?"

Removing a tissue from his pocket, Sasha wipes away the dribble of blood from his neck and says, "My relationship with Dominik is one that I will hold near and dear until I die. Whether you are worthy of the same loyalty or not, depends on you." Rising out of the chair, he makes his way to the suitcase and starts to open it. "The newest top-of-the-line weapons that haven't even been released to the public yet are inside this case."

"Then how do you have your hands on them?" I already know he probably has his fingers in all types of government offices, but hearing how honest he is in his response is what matters. Viktor joins me at my side and crosses his arms over his puffed-out chest. Reaching out, I tuck my hand into his back pocket and give his ass a nice squeeze. Leaving my hand there, I wait for Sasha to reply.

Raising an eyebrow, Sasha's eyes flicker between Viktor and me. Deciding not to comment, he finally responds to my question. "Many of my men work in national security. They keep me up-to-date on my supplies, and I keep their pockets lined with cash." Flipping the case open, he runs his hands over the seam and then turns it toward us.

Laying neatly on padding sits a variety of metal shaped into tools many like to call evil. Their calibers range from point two-two-one to point fifty, with magazines that hold various sizes of bullets, and attachments which enhance their efficiency. Interested in what I see, I walk around the table to get a better look. Turning the case toward me, I reach in and run my hand over the matte black steel. Picking up the pistol, I rotate it in my hand and test the grip placement.

"That is the Warthal PPQ. This brand-new gun hasn't reached the sights of any civilians yet but has been tested by SWAT and multiple military personnel . . ." Ding. The first lie, blocking the rest of his words out, I wrap my fingers around the grip and raise it enough so I can look through the sights.

With Sasha still rambling, I swivel my hips and focus my sights on the space between his eyes which causes him to stutter. His eyes flicker down and notice the missing magazine, but before he can get another word out, I tsk him. "Now Sasha, I thought we were going to have a trusting relationship? Surely you don't think I'm some imbecile?" Hearing my words, Frank turns his chair to the side, which gives him a clear opening to get up if needed, Viktor and Joe close their distance to me, and Sasha's guards tense.

Schooling his features, he raises an eyebrow and stoically says, "My blue fairy, I have no idea what you mean. Now, like I was saying, this weapon, when shot, is as smooth as butter and the recoil is nearly nonexistent." Out of the corner of my eye, I see Vik holding out a magazine for me to grab. Reaching back, I take it from him and quickly slam it in place and refocus on the man my father trusted.

With my voice as hard as steel, I say, "You have one more time to try me, Sasha. I like you; however, I will not be played. You are outnumbered in this room, so you might want to think before you speak again. Choose your next words wisely." With my scowl locked with his mischievous gleam, I notice from my peripheral that my men have their hands on their holsters, and their shoulders bunched from the tension; they are ready for shit to go down.

Time ticks by, and at every stroke of the secondhand, the tension grows thicker. Just before I think everyone is going to explode, Sasha's beautifully-rich laughter bellows out. Surprised, I narrow my eyes and quickly glance at everyone else and notice they are just as confused as me. Lowering the gun, I place my hand on my hip and start to tap my foot with impatience. With a sobering sigh, he finally speaks. "You, my blue fairy, are nothing like I imagined."

"Oh, really? How did you picture me then?"

"No offense, my fairy, but I expected you to be submissive and quiet. Instead, you are this fiery vixen who not only knows weapons, but you obviously know how to run the family business."

Rolling my eyes, I lay the gun back in its original place and begin to make my way out of the office. As I pass Sasha, I slap his firm ass and call over my shoulder to Viktor. "Babe, finish this for me. I gotta handle these people." With one hand on the door, I turn and lean back against it. With my gaze slowly roaming up Sasha's body, I continue, "Joe, come with me so I can get these people out here finished." My eyes finally connect with Sasha's. "Frank, stay here with Vik and make sure the pretty boy over here behaves himself."

Without waiting for their response, I turn back toward the exit and leave the office. Midway down the hall, Joe's hand comes to a rest at the dip in my back. Not missing a step, we make our way to the lounge area where people sit. People who live a life I once trudged through. But instead of piss-smelling blankets and roach-infested hotels, these people are going to be selling their bodies and fucking on fresh blankets with free condoms and a way to stay clean. Regardless of the difference, we still have one thing in common; to get anywhere in life, you have to fuck your way through it.

Their cheerful laughter slips past the main door and causes me to arch a brow. Shaking my head, I nod to Joe, who then swings the door open so hard it slams into the wall. The joy and giddiness that poured from them quickly dissolve and their moods sober up. My eyes roam over their dingy clothing and matted hair as I walk over to the railing. Leaning back against it, I draw a line with my finger in front of me. "I want ten of you to form a line." They exchange glances, but no one makes a move to do as I say. With anger surging through me, I reach over to Joe, grab his Glock, and shoot at where I want them to stand.

Screams echo throughout the steel building and shortly after, Viktor, Frank, and Sasha — who is followed by his guards — come running out with their guns at the ready. As if nothing happened, I hand Joe his Glock and cross my arms over my chest. Seeing that everything is fine, with the exception of a nice little dent in the concrete where the bullet ricocheted off, Viktor and Frank holster their weapons and turn back toward the office. Sasha and his guards, on the other hand, look like a fish out of water with their eyes wide and mouths opening and closing as if they are trying to say something but just can't formulate the words. As he nears him, Frank grips Sasha by the shoulder and turns him away from the scene I created.

Glaring at the people in front of me, I notice some with tears running down their cheeks and some visibly shaking. "Now, I'm not going to repeat this again. Ten people. NOW!" This time, my words got a reaction. Nearly everyone jumps to their feet, but once ten are in a line, the others sit back down. Straightening out, I brace my hands behind my back and slowly walk a circle around them. With each person I pass, I look them over head to toe to do a quick assessment.

Satisfied, I walk back to my spot next to Joe. "Go sit back down; the next ten come up here. We will repeat this process until everyone has come up here for me to inspect. Let me just say this. I don't give a fuck if you do drugs. Shoot up, snort, pop pills, smoke it. But if I find out anyone has overdosed while under my care, I will end that for everyone. You will *only* buy your supply from my dealer, and you will always have Narcan on your person." Glances pass back and forth, some pull down their sleeves, others nervously run their hands over their marked arms.

The inspection of all the newbies breezes by once they realize I mean business. I quickly inspect the last group and inform them they are dismissed and are to report immediately to their new living quarters. Walking away from them, I let Joe finish laying out the finer details and make my way down the stairs to where the established prostitutes moved to. To my humor, I find them all fawning over the guards who are surrounding the vehicles Sasha arrived in. At the sound of my laughter, everyone freezes. Separating from the guards, they gather together and straighten themselves out. With the single fact that they respect me enough to gather themselves without my command, I let the tension from earlier ooze from me. Cracking a smile, I walk over to them with my hand extended and the intention of getting to know them better.

Seven

THANKFULLY ALL the meetings are wrapped up in enough time for me to visit Octavia. She is weighing heavy on my mind ever since I had that fucking nightmare. With Neal still on the loose, I fear he will try to either harm her worse than what she already is or even kidnap her. After the traitorous shit he pulled, I can't put anything past him. Scowling, I shake my head and refocus on answering the mass amount of texts that seem to be pinging on my phone nonstop.

    With my fingers flying over my screen, I don't realize we are pulling up to the hospital until Frank taps me on the shoulder. Looking up from the glowing LED screen, I watch as we pull into the parking lot and take in the glowing sunset that is descending behind the nearby skyscrapers. Damn, a whole day filled with just meetings and driving. As soon as the SUV comes to a stop, I hop out and start making my way to the entrance.

Not waiting on the guys, I power walk my way into the hospital and enter an elevator. My patience is tested the entire ride to the fourth floor; the elevator stops at each floor for someone to either get on or hop off. The second the automated system indicates we're landing on the fourth floor, I shuffle to the front and surge through the sliding doors as soon as they open. With the halls clear of all nurses and patients, I make my way to the nursing station to get an update on my best friend.

The nurse who is assigned Octavia leans over her desk and starts to pick up her phone. Being the considerate person that I am, well on occasion, I wait while she dials and for the call to end. But as soon as she inputs the last number into the phone, my cell starts to ring. Frowning, I slowly reach down and pull my phone out of my pocket. Sure enough, it's the hospital. To confirm my suspicions, I answer the phone. "Hello?"

"Yes ma'am, this is Katrina, I'm Octavia's nurse for tonight—"

"Turn around Katrina." The nurses never call me, so knowing she is calling about Tavia kicks my anxiety into full gear. Before the nurse can respond, I hang up the phone. With the receiver still to her ear, Katrina turns around with a mixture of confusion and excitement. The second she notices me, she quickly hangs up the phone and speed walks over to me.

Without a word, she grabs my hand and drags me into Octavia's room. I quickly look around the room for anything amiss, but nothing catches my eye.

"I'm sorry, I didn't mean to overstep, but I

have the best news for you!" Katrina's exuberance takes me by surprise, and from her high-pitched and squeaky tone, I can tell whatever it is that's so exciting is worth it. With her hand still wrapped around mine, she pulls me over to the bed and points over to the EEG machine that is spitting out wavy lines. "This is her brain activity; ever since she went into a coma, the brain activity has been minimal; however, as of . . ." Reaching down, she threads the long strip through her hand. "Ah, here it is, as of eleven this morning, the activity has been increasing." Dropping the older section of the strip down, she runs her finger over the newest waves and looks over to me. "The waves are current. They are the same as what ours would look like right now. She should be waking up any time now!"

With every word, the pressure behind my eyes grows and with the news that she should be waking up at any moment, breaks the dam. With my gaze trained on Tavia's face, I walk around the bed and pull a chair as close as I can to where she is laying. Just as I sit down, my men finally stroll in and tense when they see tears leaking from me. Not paying them any mind, I grasp Tavia's hand with both of mine and start talking to my sleeping *chula*. "Bitch, I need you to wake up now. It hasn't been the same at the club without you. I need my drinking partner back!"

Despite hearing muffled words being exchanged between the nurse and my guys, I don't take my eyes off of her. Swiping my thumb over her hand, I focus on the steady rise of her chest. The staccato sound coming from the machines surrounding me drowns out the conversations the guys are having.

I'm not sure how long I've been sitting vigilantly at her side, but when a hand settles on my back, I jump. Turning my attention away, I look to see who it is. With a Starbucks coffee cup in his hand, Frank looks down at me in concern. Giving him a half-ass smile, I reach up for the cup containing my fuel. With it near my grasp, a twitch jerks my attention to the limp hand I'm holding. The motion happens again, but this time it is more pronounced.

I quickly stand and nearly knock the chair over in the process. Stepping closer, I lean over the side rail and run my fingers through her hair to get it off her face. With a gentle tone, I whisper, "Tavia? Can you hear me? It's me, Selene. Wake up, doll." Each word gains some kind of reaction, from scrunching her face to moving her eyes from side to side. I stand there, continuously stroking her hair, and patiently wait for her eyes to open.

Only a few seconds tick by before there is more movement. This time, however, it's her legs. They slide around under the sheets, hidden from sight. I'm sure after laying in bed for many weeks has made her stiff. As if hearing my thoughts, a grimace mars her face and her lips purse. With a flick of her tongue, she tries to wet her lips, but even that's dry.

Turning toward her bedside table, I grab the cup of ice water the nurse brought in and bring it to her mouth. "Tavia, open your mouth, I got some water for you." Again her lips pucker as if she is trying. To help her out, I dip my finger into the cup and rub the moisture onto the cracked skin. At the feeling of the moisture, she darts her tongue out once again. This time, I slide the straw into the space provided, and as if on instinct, she starts to suck down the water.

After a couple of gulps, her eyes finally start to open. Pulling the cup away, I blindly hand it over to Frank and focus my attention on my best friend. I watch her blink a few times and then she focuses on me. Instantly her confused expression leaves and slamming in its place is one of pure horror. Flinging herself forward, she grabs both my arms and starts to shake. Alarms start to go off, but that doesn't faze her; instead, she looks at me with pleading eyes and says, "Selene, you have to stop him! It's Neal! He's going to kill Dominik. He's the one who orchestrated all this! He's the one who has been beating me! All because I knew too much. He didn't want me; he wanted to use me against you. Please, you have to stop him!" Catching sight of Frank, she turns to him and continues, "Frank, you gotta stop him and Butkus! They are working together, please!"

I can't help but stand there in shock. Shit, how did I forget? Tavia was in a coma before any of the shit went down. Looking around the room, I notice all the guys are standing around nervously. Looking down to her, I slip her hands off my arms and place my palms on her cheeks. "Octavia, look at me." She keeps pleading to Frank, so to get her attention, I forcibly turn her head toward me and stare down at her. "Octavia, Dominik is dead." With those words, she freezes.

Even with my hands bracing her head, she still starts to shake it. "No, no, no, no, no! This is all my fault! I should have said something!"

"Stop it! It's not your fault! Blaming yourself won't bring him back. So calm down before the nurses have to come in here and sedate you." My threat quiets her words, but the sobs still rock through her. Letting her go, I lower the bed railing and prop myself at her side. Reaching forward, I pull her to my chest and hold her.

Rocking side to side, I soothe her sobs, and eventually, she calms. With my hands bracing her shoulders, I lean back and look her dead in her eyes. "I'm going to talk to the nurse and see if there is any way I can get you out of this place and somewhere safe."

Wiping the tears from her eyes, she nods and lays back in the bed. The whole time she is cringing with pain. Looking around, I spot her pain pump and push the button to give her more meds. Standing from her bed, I set the rail back into place and watch Tavia's eyes flutter shut. As everyone files out of the room, I hunt down the nurse to get all the arrangements taken care of. Thankfully, it doesn't take long, and less than an hour later, we are all piling back into our SUV. The things money and power can get you.

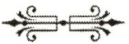

FLINGING MY keys into the bowl beside the door, I drag myself over to the large sectional and collapse down. Just as I get comfortable, my damn cell phone chirps. I let out a grumble and pull it from my back pocket to see who it is. When the screen flashes Jaime's name, I roll to the side and open his message.

J-Man: *My love, do you have any plans tonight?*
S: *Not if I have any say in it. It's been a long week. Why, what's up, babe?*
J-Man: *Would you like to join me for dinner tonight? Just the two of us?*
S: *Awe, of course! Just tell me when and where*
J-Man: *I'll be there to pick you up around six.*
S: *See you then babe <3*

With a smile plastered on my face, I roll off the couch and wrap my arms around the first body I find. Frank's bulging arms wrap over mine and pull me even closer to him. With my face pressed against his back, I breathe in his cologne and the essence that is him. His back vibrates as if he is talking, but from the constant beating of his heart and the vibrations, I don't hear a damn thing.

Leaning my head back, I say, "Ima need you to repeat that, babe, I couldn't hear you over the motor you got inside your chest."

This time when his back vibrates, it's from his laughter. Pulling me around to the front of him, I look up to him and smile right back. Lifting one hand, he strokes my cheek and says, "I said, what's got you in such a good mood?"

"Well, it has everything to do with the fact that Jaime is taking me out tonight."

His face softens at my words. Bending down, he gives me a chaste kiss and pulls away. "What time is he going to be here to get you?" His lips are still so close to mine that I can feel them slide against mine as he speaks.

Pushing up onto my toes, I press our lips together. This time instead of a chaste kiss, I deepen it. Reaching up, I thread my hands into his hair and grip it. His mouth opens with a groan that allows my tongue to invade his mouth. His roaming hands slide down to my ass, which he grips and then lifts me up. Instantly, my legs wrap around his waist, and his growing erection is directly against my core.

I am so completely lost in my amazing ass makeout session with Frank that I don't pay attention to anything else around me. So when someone clears their throat, I quickly pull back to see who it is. Viktor sits at the kitchen table with a shit-eating grin and instantly, I know it was him. Rolling my eyes, I turn back to Frank, but before I can pick up where we left off, Viktor says, "What time is your date, doll?"

My eyes stay locked on Frank as I reply, "Six, why?"

"You might want to hold off on fucking the old man for a bit. It's five twenty-three and knowing you, you are going to need all those minutes to get ready." Letting out a grunt, Frank slowly lowers me back to the floor and then reaches down to readjust himself.

With a promise to pick up from where we left off, I turn toward the front door, so I can head to my apartment. Just as I close their door, I overhear "cockblocker" and "lucky fucker" being tossed around. With a final tug, I close the door the rest of the way and shake my head at their antics.

Eight

I HAVE no idea where Jaime plans on taking me tonight, so I quickly shower and shave. Once all the suds are rinsed off, I speed out of the shower nearly busting my ass on the slick tiles. Thankfully, I gain my balance back in the nick of time and snatch the towel off the rack. Speeding out of the bathroom, I pat myself off and start to skim my closet for what I should wear.

I'm not sure how many times my eyes skimmed over the selection before I give up. Tossing my hair into a towel bun, I grab my phone from my bed and shoot a message over to Jaime, asking what he suggests. While I wait for his response, I don my undergarments and lather down in lotion. Just as I start to walk into the bathroom, my phone dings. All he replies back is "comfortable." Well shit. That doesn't help much! I can be comfortable naked, in a pair of sweatpants, or a sundress. Letting out a sigh of frustration, I quickly tap my reply and toss my phone back onto the bed.

He doesn't wanna give me more details, fine. Walking back to my closet, I pull out a pair of distressed capris, tan flats, and an off-the-shoulder jersey tee. It only takes a second to pull everything on, so I am left with a good amount of time to do my hair and makeup. Deciding to keep with the casual attire, I apply some neutral tones and keep my hair down so it can dry into its natural waves. A knock on my door causes me to scramble to finish.

Just as I spritz myself with some perfume, another knock sounds at this door. I open my mouth to yell out there, but the click of the door opening causes me to pause. With a final look in the mirror, I grab my phone and stroll out of my room. "About time you let yourself in. I've only told you like what, ten times now to get a copy of my apartment key." I might as well have been talking to my phone because the whole time I was speaking, that's where I was looking.

However, doing that wasn't my smartest decision, because the voice that responds back has me looking up from my phone in surprise. "My, my. If I had known it was that easy to get in, I would have been here sooner." The deep and sensual tone Sasha just gave me causes a chill to overtake me. Noticing the reaction he gave me, he flashes me a seductive grin that only makes the sexual tension between us grow. Frozen in place, I watch as he makes his way over to me. His movements are full of swagger, but his eyes say something different—they blaze as if he is starving and I'm the prey.

He is nearly toe to toe with me before the

ringing of my phone grabs my attention. With my eyes locked on his, I take a few steps back to compose myself. After a few deep breaths, I finally check my phone and notice it's Jaime.

"Well, hello my *papi chulo*."

"*Mi amor*, I just wanted to let you know I'm down the street. I know you like taking your time to get ready."

"Well how the table has turned, I'm actually waiting on you."

Letting out a chuckle and a content sigh, he replies, "I'll see you soon, my love. Stay feisty!"

After giving him a kiss through the phone, I hang up and shove it back in my pocket. Looking back at Sasha, he meets my gaze and arches his brow. Shaking my head, I turn him by his shoulders and push him toward the door. "You can't stay. I have somewhere to be, and you aren't invited."

"Are you sure about that? You don't want to pick up where we left off?" His rich accent caresses me in ways I enjoy entirely too much. "I have other things you can try. The tricks my tongue can do, and I'm sure I have something that will make you scream." Fuck, his voice is so fucking husky and laced with lust.

I push him all the way to the door without saying a single word. I don't trust my voice, and I know the second I say anything, he will know the effect his presence has on me. We finally reach the entrance, and just as soon as I let up on the pressure from pushing him, he snatches my wrist and pulls me in front of him. Taking a step back, I run into the door and freeze. Fuck.

His fiery gleam only shines brighter as I try

to slide out from in front of him, but before I can even get anywhere, his arms box me in, and he is completely against me. Tilting my head back to scowl at him, I find myself only a breath's distance from his lips. If I were to lick mine, I would touch his, and even though I want to, it's not going to happen. Not even if the feeling of his fucking dick pressing against my abdomen feels amazing.

Raising my hands, I brace them on his chest and push. "Look, it's not going to happen. Yes, you're sexy as hell, but I love them. Plus, five dicks are enough."

Dropping his arms, he sighs and grunts. "It may not happen now, but baby, you know we need to happen. Until then, I'll be around." The moment he steps back from me, all the heat surging my body leaves.

Shaking my head, I turn and open the door only to find Jaime on the other side. Letting out a squeal, I jump into his arms and wrap my legs around him. "God, I missed you, J. Don't stay away for so long!" I don't care if I'm pouting or what Sasha is thinking right now, this is my man, and I haven't seen him in a couple of weeks.

With one arm holding me, he threads his fingers through my waves and smashes my lips to his. Our kiss is full of apologies and the urgency to be together. Our tongues slide against each other, and I suck on his full lips which makes him groan. With our lips still locked, he carries me into my apartment and sits me on the counter. His hands glide up my waist and onto my breasts where he rubs his thumb over the top of my peaked nipples. Frustrated from the shirt keeping up apart, he lifts it up to take it off.

Pulling back from him, I catch a very attentive Sasha propped against the wall watching everything going on as if he is watching a live-action porno. Squeezing my arms down, I stop Jaime in his tracks. He starts to protest, so I grasp his jaw and turn his attention to our audience. "Who the fuck is that?" Jaime's jaw clenches underneath my grip, and I can see his eyes dilate with aggravation.

Straightening from the wall, Sasha pulls a hand from his pocket and extends it in greetings. "My name is Sasha. I'm Selene's—"

I have no idea what he is planning on saying, so I quickly cut him off, "He's my business partner. That's it. He was actually just leaving when you arrived, love." Sensing the finality of my tone, Sasha balls his hand up and shoves it back into his pocket. Flicking my attention over to Jaime, I see he is puffed up with his arms crossed over his chest. His sleeves are damn near being ripped apart from his hulking biceps.

"I think that's a smart idea. Here, let me escort you out." Jaime is basically growling as he talks and without even waiting for a response from Sasha, he stomps over to the front door, swings it open, and points. "Leave."

Nodding his head goodbye to me, Sasha takes a few steps back and then turns on his heel. The whole time, Jaime has his scowl locked on him, stalking the man who dares to step foot into my home. I can't help but shake my head and smile at how territorial he is being. Hell, I find it a little bit cute.

Sasha is barely out the door before Jaime slams it shut. Not bothering to see if it injured him, Jaime prowls over to me and slides in between my legs. Delving his hands underneath my shirt, he reaches up and pinches my nipples, making me jump. Through a devious smile, he says, "Now, where were we?"

Fighting against a moan, I grasp his wrist and pull it from under my shirt and put it up against my lips. "I believe you promised me a date." With a kiss to his wrist, I release it and start to slide off the counter.

With a reluctant sigh, he helps me off the counter and kisses the top of my head. "That I did, I hope you are ready for a little drive."

"How far is a little?"

"No more than thirty minutes." With a slap on the ass, he walks off and opens the door for me. "Whenever you're ready, *mi amor*." Instead of the scowl, he gives me a dimple-popping smile. Not wanting to cause any reason for that dimple to hide, I grab my wallet and waltz out the door with Jaime following right behind me.

Thankfully, Sasha has cleared the hall. Where he could go in such a short time beats me, but if I had to guess, I would say he is pestering Frank, Joe, Viktor, and Godfrey in their apartment. Not wanting to cause any further delays, I bypass their door and enter the elevator that Jaime is holding open for me. As soon as I walk in, Jaime pulls me over to him, turns my back toward him and wraps his arms around me. With my head leaning back against his chest, I close my eyes and let his warmth soak into me.

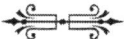

WE'VE BEEN on the road for nearly thirty minutes now with the radio blasting a mix of Spanish and hip-hop music. The bass booms with the beat and my hips sway in the seat. Jaime's Shelby GT500 purrs like no other, it's a beast, just like its owner. The interior is all black which stands in contrast to the white exterior and to make it pop; there are neon blue lights illuminating the accents.

Another great song starts to play, so I let the beat sink into me, but just as the intro starts, Jaime reaches over and turns the volume down. With a hand on the shifter, he looks over to me with a smirk and says, "As much as I would love to ride around jamming out to music with you, *mi amor*, we are a couple of minutes away. My *madre* knows everyone, and if they tell her we blasted music down their street, she will take a *chancla* to my ass."

Sitting up in my seat, I look at him in horror. "Wait! We are meeting your mom? You didn't tell me that! I would have dressed nicer! Jaime, not fair! I call foul!" Holy shit, I've never met anyone's parents—like ever. So knowing that I'm going over there as his girlfriend puts on a whole new level of stress I've never dealt with before. Frantically, I start to straighten out my hair and cover any line of cleavage showing.

Reaching over, Jaime grabs my hand and pulls it up to his lips. "I didn't tell you because I know you wouldn't have come. She has been on my case for a couple of years now to meet someone, and now that I have you, I think it's time for her to meet you." With a kiss to the back of my hand, he releases it, downshifts the car, and turns into a driveway.

Whipping my head around, I take in my surroundings. With the only light outside being the moon, not much is visible. The house we pulled up to is a Spanish style home with a perfectly manicured lawn, a two-car garage, and a yard full of people. "Jaime. What if they know me . . ." I can't keep my eyes off the abundant amount of people walking around. Some with plates of food, others with Coronas, and some with kids on their hip. Shit.

"It's gonna be fine, just wait. If anyone says anything to you, let me know. I'll handle it." Jaime sounds so calm and nonchalant about everything. Oddly enough, it makes my anxiety so much worse. How can I be perfectly okay with thousands of people seeing my pussy and many of them have had their fingers inside of me, but coming here shakes me to the core?

The sound of his door opening makes me jump in my seat. Whirling around, I watch as he climbs out, closes his door, and makes his way around the car to my side. Before I think to lock myself inside, he has my door open. The music that pours from inside the house slides into my ears and drowns out the thud of my heart. Jaime reaches a hand out to me and holds it there. He doesn't rush or scowl at me; instead, he patiently waits.

I would stay hidden in the car forever if not for all the eyes that are turning our way. Taking a deep breath, I place my hand in his and slide out of my hiding spot. With his arm draped over my hip, Jaime leads me up the paved path to the house. Nearly halfway up the walkway, I finally take my eyes off the path and look up. Relief overwhelms me as I notice that no one is focusing on me. Yeah, there are side-eyes and quick glances here and there, but that's about all I get.

We make it up the two stairs leading to the door, but as soon as we step onto the porch, someone calls out Jaime's name. "Jaime! *Jefe* is that you?" A husky man who carries a Corona walks over and takes a closer look. "*SI!* Jaime, it's been a long time! *Dónde has estado?*" Reaching out, he pulls Jaime in for a hug and pats his back with enthusiasm. Clasping my hands behind my back, I stay quiet and watch their interaction.

I don't think I've ever seen Jaime have such a legit smile like he does now. It takes him a few seconds to process who it is that's talking to him, but the second it clicks, he becomes highly animated. Speaking in Spanish, I can only catch the small words; usually, it's just numbers and occasionally the word pain. Not wanting to be rude, I let my eyes roam over all the people crowding the front porch. What should only comfortably hold three to four people is now holding at least ten. Everyone's skin tone ranges from a pale caramel to a rich umber.

I take in the luscious curves the women have and the cocky attitudes most of the men exude. Their laughter fills the air, and with every passing second, my anxiety starts to ease. The sound of my name makes me return my focus back to Jaime. With a nod of his head, he motions for me to come closer. Now by his side, he wraps his arm around my waist and tucks his hand into my back pocket.

"Selene, this is Carlos, my cousin, and Carlos, this is Selene, my lady." At Jaime's introduction, I reach my hand out to shake his, but instead, Carlos pulls me into a tight hug. Shocked by his action, it takes me a minute to return it. But as my arms wrap around his a feeling of acceptance sounds in me. Finally, after what seems like forever, but in reality was just a couple seconds, he lets me go.

Safely wrapped in Jaime's arm, I start to pull my phone out to check the cause of the constant vibration in my pocket, but before I can even slip it out of my pocket, Carlos questions me. "So Selene, how did you meet *mi amigo*? Last I heard he spent all his time with the FBI."

I can't help but smirk at his question. Do I tell him the truth? That Jaime and his now-dead partner were investigating gang activity? That I'm a mafia boss, and my territory is spread throughout the surrounding cities? Naw, I'll keep the juicy details between Jaime and I. Instead I think up a generic answer. "He was in —"

I'm unable to finish giving my answer because a loud voice overpowers me. Looking over my shoulder, I see a short, plump elderly woman shuffling through the door with a sandal in her hand. "*Jaime Maximiliano Mantilla! Donde tú haz estado! Nunca llamas y hace un año que no estás en casa! Ni siquiera haz ido a la iglesia. Respondeme muchacho!*"

With the way she waves the sandal, I start to step to the side, but Jaime maneuvers me so that

I'm standing in front of him. Scowling over my shoulder, I start to scold him, but his nervous expression makes me pause. Looking back at the lady, I nearly scream because she is almost on top of me. Taking a step back, I get a better look at her and notice the very similar features that Jaime has. Just like that, it all clicks. Fuck, this is his mom!

Nine

WHY DID I not think about this? I feel like a fish out of water with no way to breathe. This petite woman comes no higher than my shoulders, and yet, she is scary as hell. She looks like the kind of woman who would drag a grown man by his ear and pull him over her knee for spankings. Shit, what if she does that to Jaime? I think I might just die . . . from laughter! Her scowl accentuates all of the creases that mark her face, her box-dyed red curls bounce from shaking the flipflop at Jaime, and she is doing this weird thing where she clicks her dentures together. Without a doubt, she is pissed.

I start taking small steps back so that she doesn't notice me, but Jaime grips my hip harder and drags me back in front of him as if I'm his shield. Jabbing my elbow back, I connect with his stomach and hear him oomph in response. Looking down at the intimidating woman, I plaster a smile on my face. Her squinty eyes meet mine, and just as I think she is about to lay the smackdown on me, she flicks her attention over my shoulder to her little chickenshit behind me.

Everyone surrounding us is either whispering or silently watching the scene unfold. Hell, I know if I weren't in the middle of it, I would probably be doing the same thing. Instead, I'm being used as a human shield to hide a massive man from his mama. This time when I step to the side, I quickly step out of Jaime's reach, which leaves him wide open. His mom doesn't hesitate and quickly pops him on his chiseled chest. The pop from the sandal hitting him echoes on the porch, causing multiple people, including myself, to groan in sympathy. The words flying out of her mouth are so fast that I can't even pick up the slightest bit of them. All I know is she is pissed, and Jaime just keeps his head bowed. Almost as if he was a child who broke an expensive vase.

The second she pauses, Jaime raises his hands in surrender and says, "Mama, I'm sorry. I should have called. Work has been busy, and when I'm not working, I'm with my girlfriend. Please calm down; you know your heart can't handle it." Aw, I've never been called anyone's girlfriend before. Not even by one of the other guys. I don't know why, but it makes me like Jaime a little more than I already do.

At his words, the vicious woman turns her glare toward me. This time, instead of squinting at me, she openly takes in my appearance. Under her scrutiny, I start to fiddle my fingers. She makes me nervous in ways I have never been before. The silence almost breaks me, but just before it does, she finally speaks. "Jaime, *ella es hermosa!*" Heat flames on my cheeks at her words. I know what they mean. She thinks I'm beautiful.

"*Mamá, ella no habla español. Por favor habla en inglés.*" He looks to me in apology, but I just shrug my shoulders. I haven't mentioned that I know a little Spanish, so his apology isn't really needed. However, I am glad he asked for English. Carrying on a long conversation in Spanish would stump me.

Rolling her eyes, she waves Jaime off and continues to focus on me. Her little feet shuffle forward until she is now standing right against me. As much as I don't want to, I have to look down to her in order to maintain our eye contact. Her arm shoots up, startling me, but to my surprise, she gently lays her palm against my cheek. "You are beautiful. Thank you for taking care of my boy." The love pouring from her is more than I can handle, so I melt into the warmth of her hand.

The onlookers must have taken her gesture as a sign of peace, because their chatter picks up again, along with the music and laughter. Dropping her hand, she grabs mine and starts to tug me along behind her as she walks back into the house. Not wanting to get on her bad side, I follow along, but not without glancing back to ensure Jaime is following too. As we walk past the front door, the music becomes muffled, but the number of people increases. I'm not sure how we are even going to try to walk through without being trampled.

To my surprise, everyone parts like the Red

Sea, which allows us to maneuver our way to an empty kitchen table. Releasing my hand, she pulls out her chair at the head oval table and motions for me to sit beside her. With my ass firmly planted in the seat, I tuck my hands under the table, reach over to Jaime's thigh, and grip. Bastard might be cute, but he dragged me out here without letting me prepare first.

Waving her hand, Jaime's mom gets the attention of one of the passing guys, holds up three fingers and nods to the guy when he said something. I didn't hear what he said over all the other talking but with the gleam on the exiting man's face, I know they are up to no good. With her attention back on me again, she looks me over and says, "What's your name, girl?"

"Selene, Selene Romanov. And what might yours be? Since Jaime is being a bad son by not introducing us." The second my last name left my lips, recognition flashed across her face.

"Romanov, ay? Tell Dominik that Luciana said hello."

"As much as I would love to, I'm not able to pass your message on."

"And why is that *nina*? Is he even too busy for you? The street rat he turned into a *princessa*?"

Clicking my tongue, I roll my eyes are her sarcastic response and stomp down the smart-ass response that I'm fighting to let out. Instead, I plaster a smile and practically snarl. "No. He was murdered so unless you know how to summon spirits, he won't be replying back to you." As much as I tried to keep my anger at bay, I couldn't stop it from leaking out. Luciana's eyes are nearly as large as saucers. Thankfully, that random guy returns carrying three shot glasses of clear liquor and a bowl containing salt and lemons. Not waiting for anyone else, I reach out and snag a shot. Before I can even take another breath, the cool liquid flows down my throat.

With my glass empty, I can only eyeball the other two shots remaining. Sensing my inner turmoil, Jaime pushes his shot over to me and softly says, "Here *hermosa*, have mine. I'm the driver tonight. What kind of agent would I be if I drink and drive."

Snorting, I lift his shot glass to my lips and mutter a snarky response. "Like that's the worst thing you've ever done!" Sliding his now empty glass back toward him, I turn my attention back to Luciana and laugh at her bemused expression.

Nodding her head to the last shot, she gives me permission to finish them off. Grabbing the last shot glass, I don't question her nor do I care. I don't even care that I'm using the liquor to cover up the pain of Dominik being brought up. With all the glasses now empty, I casually start to scope the area and all the people surrounding us.

"So Selene, how did you meet my boy? Are you the reason he hasn't been home in nearly a year?" The low blow to Jaime doesn't get missed by me and by the look on Jaime's face, it didn't get past him either.

With three shots weighing heavily on my empty stomach, I throw caution to the wind and answer her bluntly. "As much as I would love to take all the blame for his absence, we've only known each other for a couple of months now. So the rest of the time is on him to explain."

Letting out a hmph, Luciana clicks her

tongue and points her acrylic nail at Jaime. "You better have an excuse, boy. I didn't carry you around for nine months and then wipe your ass for all those years just for you to forget about your madre."

"*Lo siento mamá, te lo compensaré!* My next day off I'll come get you and spend the day with you. *Si?*"

"That next day off better not be next year or else I'll find you and drag you out by your ear." As hard as she tried to stay serious, she can't fight the smirk that is pushing its way through. Rising from her seat, she walks over to Jaime and wraps her arms around his head which smothers his face in her over-abundant bosom. With a kiss to the top of his head, she lets him go. "Now shoo, y'all go enjoy yourselves."

Jaime is quickly out of his chair and motions for me to hurry. Raising a brow, I make sure to take my time to stand from the chair, but once I'm upright, he has his hand in mine, and he starts to tug me along. As we start to walk into the living room, his mom calls out for me. Looking back to her, I see her hands clasped over her heart. "Take care of *mi hijo*."

Shaking my hand out of Jaime's, I walk back over to his mom and wrap her in my arms. "I will do all I can in my power to keep him safe. I promise you." Little does she know, my power reaches far and wide. So as long as he stays loyal to the cause, keeping him safe will be a breeze. Pulling back, I kiss her cheek and then make my way back over to Jaime. With our fingers once again intertwined, I start to walk only to feel resistance. Looking back in confusion, I take in

Jaime staring at me. Not just any normal stare, no, he has that look. If we were living in a cartoon world, I'm sure cupid would be flying nearby with his bow minus an arrow.

Closing the distance between us, I wrap my arms around his waist and raise to my tiptoes. "What's that look for?" Shaking his head, he doesn't answer me; instead, he bends down and claims my lips. Our kiss may be quick, but it doesn't lack the passion that his eyes were screaming. Pulling away from him, I go to his side and take a few subtle deep breaths. The amount of . . . love coming from Jaime is overwhelming, and I honestly don't know how to handle it. I haven't gotten there with him yet and to know he is waiting for me to meet him at that line is kinda scary.

Lost in thought, I blindly follow him through the house. Every now and then he stops and greets family and friends — making sure to introduce me to them in the process. By the third person, I finally have that L word pressed to the back of my mind. Spotting a minibar, I lead us over to it and start to pour myself a mixed drink of Dr. Pepper and Fireball. With a full solo cup in hand, we head out the back door to where it looks like the life of the party is.

The music is thumping back here, and it reminds me of Sub Rosa. Since Dominik's death, I haven't been able to enjoy the club like I used to. Humming in approval, I start to sway to the beat and playfully dance around Jaime. Without needing further encouragement, he leads me onto the grass where a mass of bodies are grinding and swaying to the tempo to the music.

We easily make our way to the center of the crowd and join the wave of bodies. Turning my back toward Jaime, I dance against him and let the warmth of his body soak into me. His hands roam all over me, and when they reach my hands, he spins me in circles.

With each spin or rotation, I get a chance to take in my surroundings. Aside from the glow of the moon, there are four ropes of light that come from each corner of the yard and meet in the middle, giving enough brightness to help prevent us from trampling each other. The music filling our souls is coming from the two speakers that are facing each other on opposite sides of the yard — each one standing nearly as tall as me. Up against the back of the house, there is a grill lit in a full blaze, and to the left of it, there are four coolers full of drinks.

By the sixth — maybe seventh — song, I signal to Jaime that I'm done for a bit, and we make our way over to those oh-so-inviting coolers. My cup was empty early into the dancing, so I toss it in the hefty black trash bag and then search the coolers for something to takes its place. Bingo! Ice-cold water. Pulling two bottles out, I toss one to Jaime and quickly twist my top off. I'm about halfway done with my bottle when a curvy woman walks past Jaime and then stops to do a double take. I don't even have my lid back on my bottle by the time she has her arms wrapped around my man. Anger instantly flares through me, and once she turns to the side, insecurity joins the party. She is not only curvy as all fucking get out, but her belly is rounded by a growing crotch goblin.

Even with all my raging emotions, I take my time creeping closer, but what she says has all those negative emotions instantly gone. "¡*Primo! ¿Cómo estás?*" Cousin. Shit, that coulda been bad. Pregnant or not, I would have snatched a bitch over my man. Shaking my head, I finish walking over to Jaime and idle up beside him. Spotting me out of the corner of his eye, he wraps an arm around me and continues his conversation with her.

Not wanting to eavesdrop on their conversation, I let my focus stray to all the passing people and the sky that is a blanket of sparkling stars and darkness. But out of the corner of my eye, I notice Jaime placing his hand on his cousin's rounded belly. "Bella, what's this?"

Bemusement and awe are evident in his voice, but upon hearing his question, I can't help but answer for her with a sarcastic-ass response. "It's a dinosaur, duh!" Finding myself hilarious, I burst out laughing and luckily Bella thinks it's funny as well because she joins in with my rib-cracking laugh. Hell, we laugh so hard she braces herself on my arm, and we both end up wiping tears away as we finally settle down.

With her hand still on my arm, Bella looks me once over and smiles brightly. "I like you *chica*. Stick around for a while. *Si?*"

Nodding my head, I return her cheeky grin and give Jaime a hip bump. Looking up to him, I can't help but gloat. "You hear that, Suave, they like me. Me and Bella here are gonna become best friends so watch out!"

Ten

WE STAY at the party until midnight rolls around and as we leave, I make sure to exchange numbers with not only Bella but Luciana as well. This time on the way home, we don't have the radio blaring; instead, we sit in each other's company and let the quiet vibrations from the V8 overtake us.

During the ride, I can't help but take quick glances at Jaime. Bringing me to his family's house and meeting everyone brought a whole new perspective to the light. I'm so lucky that this man came knocking on my door. Hell, I'm lucky he felt such a strong connection between us to change his life for me. I mean, not only did he kill his partner for my trust—not that he didn't need it—but he also keeps Frank and the others informed about the intel coming from the FBI. Not only is his career on the line, but so is his life.

Part of me thinks he is crazy as shit for risking everything, but I mean love is a good reason, right? Lost in the vicious cycle of wanting to know, I lean my head back and roll it to the side, so I am looking at him dead on. "Jaime, what makes me worth it all?"

Scrunching his face, he quickly looks back from me and the road a couple of times and then grunts his response, "Because for the first time in my life, I met a woman who takes my breath away and at the same time, takes no shit from anyone. The first time we met, I got a good look in your eyes, and I saw the scars and dark shadows that lay in there, but I also saw your pure heart. I knew that if I could get a chance to love you, you would make it worthwhile and something I would never regret."

"Not a single day has gone by where I regret my decision. The thought doesn't even cross my mind. Yeah, I may lose my career, but in the end, knowing that I got a chance to hold you and call you mine is worth it. I was living day by day and not giving a shit if I even made it home. There was no one waiting on me, no one to warm the space next to me in bed, and with a toxic relationship from Butkus, I was starting to hate myself. So knocking on your door was like some greater power knocking on my mind telling me to wake up and look what's in front of me. That something . . . was you."

Well shit. His confession makes my heart do this weird flutter, and then it swells. I know what I'm feeling is love, but I know it's too soon to tell him. I want to be in love with him when I do. Yeah, I knew the others a couple of months more than him, but with them, I knew it was real. So instead of rejecting what he said, I bottle up all the love he is filling me with and tuck it close. When the time is right, I'll let it out, and I'll mean it with all I am.

Instead of replying to him, I reach over, grab his hand, and bring it to my lips. After a soft kiss to his knuckles, I move his hand to my lap and lazily run my thumb over it. Looking over to him, I catch his eyes and just express with my look, what I'm feeling. I don't know if he understands or knows how to read me yet, regardless I hold nothing back. With a wink, he looks back to the road and drives us back to my place where I ask him to stay. I may not want to confess what I'm feeling verbally, but there's nothing wrong with playing charades in bed.

The sexual tension is like a rubber band being stretched to the max, and as soon as we make it to my floor, we snap. We are both in a lust-induced fog with magnets attached to our bodies. I quickly find myself plastered against him, and god, it feels amazing. With the height difference and his hulking form, I fit against him like a puzzle piece. My hands trail up his corded muscles until they reach his neck where I drag him down to me. Our lips hover apart from each other for only a brief second, and then all restraint is lost. Even with how ravenous we are for each other, the second our mouths collide I feel nothing but raw emotions.

We don't separate until we have my door open and the second we have it closed, we start to strip. As we make our way to the room, clothes go all over the place—on the back of the couch, on the floor, and even the end table. By the time we make it to my bed, I'm only in my bra and panties. Just as I reach back to unlatch lacy material that is holding my breasts, Jaime closes the distance and presses himself against me.

The feeling of his silky dick pressing against my ass makes me arch back against him to get some kind of friction. Needing to be closer to him, I quickly unsnap my bra and toss it to the side. Jaime's hands quickly replace the lacy material and cup my full breasts. With daunting fingers, he grips both my nipples and tweaks them hard enough to cause me to suck air through my teeth. His hands release my throbbing nubs and start their trail down my body. His touch is light and delicate as if he was rubbing a feather over fragile crystal glass. In their wake, a trail of goosebumps erupt.

The lazy path his hands travel leaves me in stimulus overload. I'm whimpering with need, and my channel is drenched, so when he reaches the seam of my matching lace panties, I nearly lose it. He doesn't dip underneath the material or even glide over the top of it. No, he tortures me by running his fingers in a line on the seam. In a huff of frustration, I lean my head back against his shoulder and lull my head to the side. I instantly regret it because Jaime bends down and nips my ear lobe and then blows air on the sensitive skin just behind my ear. Tilting my head to the side, I capture his mouth and pour my sexual frustration into the frantic kiss.

My need to be filled must have registered with him because he finally slides beneath my underwear and shoves two of his fingers into my aching pussy. My gasp is swallowed up, and my moans are muffled behind Jaime's plush lips. His fingers are relentless as they pump into me. They curl deliciously inside me, and with every thrust, they stroke over that lovely little spot that most men always forget about. Slipping his hand further in my panties, he now has access to his thumb, which he quickly puts to work stroking my clit. The dual stimulation drives me to my peak, and just as my orgasm explodes, he stops.

I start to whimper and wiggle against him, but I freeze as I hear the sound of material ripping. Looking down, I see my favorite pair of panties, now in two pieces. Jaime's husky voice draws my attention back to him. "You ain't gonna cum on my fingers; I want your pussy pulsating around my cock when you do." I swear if I was made of ice, I would melt.

Not wanting to lose the pre-orgasmic bliss, I forget about the destroyed panties and quickly crawl onto the bed. Flipping to my back, I bask in the burning gaze that is raking across my body. "Come on then, *papi*, show me what you're working with." Jaime arches a brow at me before he makes his way over.

As he climbs closer to me, he plants a mixture of kisses and nibbles in a trail that leads straight to my drenched pussy. "You are so fucking sexy Selene, *te amo mi amor*." His delicious Latin accent curls around me and nearly makes me purr. When he reaches the apex of my thighs, he moves so that he is hovering just above my slit and inhales my sweet scent.

This slow and torturous thing Jaime is doing isn't what I'm used to; I'm not patient enough for him to take his time. Wanting him to fucking devour me already, I tilt my pelvis up and try to grind on his face. I only get myself lifted off the bed before he has an arm draped over my waist to hold me down. With his other hand, he trails his fingers down my thigh and over my swollen lips, where he parts them and exposes my glistening pearl.

I hold my breath in anticipation as I watch him duck his head and take the first swipe. As soon as he makes contact, my nerve endings explode, making a needy moan escape me. Collapsing down onto the soft material below me, I get lost in the rhythmic sensations Jaime is causing. My legs start to quiver as I near the breaking point once again, not wanting him to stop, I reach down and run my fingers through his buzzed cut hair and hold his face down so he can't pull away.

Just as I think I'm going to reach the heavenly abyss, he fucking bites my clit, causing me to throw my hands up which allows him to move away. Letting out a frustrated groan, I prop myself up on my elbows and glower down at him. "If you keep leaving me hanging, I'm going to go get one of the guys and have them finish me off!" My threat must have hit a nerve because as soon as the last word slips past my lips, he's on top of me.

Dropping back down on the bed, I wrap my arms around him and start to run my nails up and down his rippling back. Pulling him down, he starts to kiss his way from my neck up to my jaw, and finally, our lips join in a frenzied battle. The smooth ministrations of his tongue coax moans out of me and with each one, his dick twitches. The head of his member is hovering right above my slit, just begging to impale me.

Jaime leans up and wraps his hand around his dick and nudges my outer lips apart, revealing my gushing pussy. He starts to run his dick up and down to get it lubricated, but he is going so slow I get impatient and grate out, "Just fucking spit on it and fuck me!" Fire licks through my veins in both anger and lust.

With his eyes still locked on where we are touching, he retorts, "Nah baby, I want your sweet juices covering my dick." His eyes are scrunched in concentration, and when his member is lathered from base to tip, he slowly sinks into my waiting channel. My pussy stretches around his girth and by the time he bottoms out, I'm a withering mess. Propping himself up on his forearms, he lays his forehead against mine and lets out a breath. "You're so fucking tight wrapped around me like a vice grip."

"Shut up and fuck me, *papi*!" I love his Spanish accent, but fuck I need to get off. On that note, I wrap my legs around his waist and give him a squeeze to spur him on. His hips finally start to move in a slow pistoning motion. With every in and out motion, he slides across that soft spot where all my nerves are hidden. I mewl into his mouth, and after so many ministrations, I start to become frenzied and blurt out, "Harder and faster! Stop teasing me!" To show I mean it, I draw his lip in between my teeth and bite. The taste of iron burst on my tongue, and when I release it, I see the blood start to pool.

Flicking his tongue out, Jaime licks the droplet away and then looks to me in shock. I can't help but smirk at him. Serves him right for teas— "Ohhh fuck yes!!" Jaime's crooked smile is the only thing I see as I open my eyes. His pelvis slams into mine with such a force it's making the whole bed shake. His intensity is sudden and unexpected, but fuck, I'm not complaining. Instead, I moan encouragements, egging him on to fuck me harder.

My orgasm that he kept hanging in front of me is now within grasping reach, so not knowing if he is going to stop again, I roll us so that I'm on top and I start riding him like a fucking cowgirl. In this position, his dick goes even deeper and bumps against my cervix every time I slam myself down. Swiveling my hips with each downward thrust, I bring that orgasm I've been chasing closer and closer. Throwing my head back, I let my wavy turquoise hair cascade down my back, and I reach up to tweak my nipples.

Pleasure shoots down my body, straight to my core with each pinch and with a final twist, I finally explode. A scream rips from me, and I nearly black out from the fucking euphoria. Below me, Jaime is still pumping his hips which only prolongs my orgasm, and just as he starts to lose rhythm, he reaches down and starts to strum my swollen clit. I can't even recover from my first orgasm before another one quickly climbs and detonates. My pussy is clenching around his cock, and as my second orgasm peaks, he lets out a roar.

Jaime stills beneath me and grips my hips with such strength; his nails bite into my skin. Collapsing onto his chest, I get lost in the combination of our erratically beating hearts, our deep inhalations, and the twitching of his dick as it empties its contents into my channel. I'm not sure how long we laid like this, but eventually, my breathing slows, and my heart is beating at its normal pace. Jaime's fingers lazily run up and down my back, drawing swirls and small circles. Planting a small kiss on his chest, I lift myself off of him and roll to the side of the bed.

My legs shake as I stand from the bed, but I fight the urge to stay laying in bed. My body is sticky from our sexual escapade, and after dancing at the party, a shower is much needed. To make matters worse, as I make my way to the bathroom, fluid mixed with his seed and my juices slowly starts to make its way down my thigh. I stop in the doorway and look over my shoulder to where Jaime is laying to find him staring at me with hooded eyes. Calling out to him, "You can join me if you want." Not waiting for his reply, I saunter over to the shower and turn it on.

When the water a nearly scalding, I step in and let the almost lava-like water flow over me. The sound of Jaime sucking in a breath catches my attention and makes me turn. Standing just outside the reach of the water, he stands with his toes curled and leaning away from the spray. "Fuck, how can you stand that! It's like *fuego!*" I can't help but laugh at him and the way he is acting. Making matters worse, I splash him causing him to jump back to avoid getting burned.

He scowls at me and turns to leave, but instead, I give in and turn the heat down. "There, I cooled it off for ya, *papi*, now come in here and wash me."

"You're the devil woman; I don't know how you do it. Now hand me the rag, let me clean that pretty ass of yours."

During the shower, we fucked twice and had to rewash ourselves all over again. When the water got cold, we migrated back to the bed and continued our escapades all night long. We didn't slow down and get ready for sleep until the sun started peaking over the horizon, and by then, we were just as dirty as before the shower. With more cum running down my thigh, I scoot into Jaime's arms and throw a blanket over us. Wrapping an arm around me, Jaime leans down and kisses me slowly one last time. When we separate, he whispers, "Good night *mi amor,* get some sleep."

Eleven

IT'S BEEN a week since Jaime's confession, and I'm still reeling. I find myself no longer keeping him at arm's distance; instead, I'm pulling him closer. Frank is no longer as standoffish with him, and Godfrey broke the silence between them. I guess they were waiting for some kind of sign he wasn't playing me this whole time. Not only have my relationships improved, but I've also practically gained a new mother overnight. Luciana has called me every day just to see how I'm doing; our conversations range from short general check-in to nearly two hours long. Let me not forget Bella, Jaime's cousin. She's been texting me like crazy, and from her last text, I've been invited to her baby shower. I have never been to one of those.

Everything that has been going on is like a whirlwind. Frank, Joe, Viktor, and Godfrey don't have any family to share with me. So being able to share this with Jaime is more than I even imagined. The only family I have is Octavia and the guys, but it's nothing like having a mother figure. Even with all the changes, I don't think I've been this happy since prior to . . . well, prior to Dominik's death.

Aside from that, Octavia is back at her house now instead of being stuck in the hospital. She is undergoing two types of therapy to help her get back to her regular self, and I hired a nurse to care for her twenty-four seven. Everything is finally looking up so with a positive disposition, I arrive at Sub Rosa early and start working on the things that need my attention. Like the overflowing stack of papers that now crowd my desk. You would think that the mafia would be paperless to prevent leaving a paper trail. But it's totally the opposite. I have receipts for everything, detailed reports of incidents that happened in the club, and a flow of requests from not only the staff but from civilians asking from some kind of job to be completed. This would be so much easier for me if I had a secretary, but after what Neal did . . . It's just too hard to trust anyone these days.

I'm nearly done with inputting the last job request when someone knocks on my office door. I quickly glance over to the security monitors that are to the left and notice it's David. "Come in!"

"Boss, I got a Michael Diaz on the line, he claims he is part of that gang that we have had our eyes on. From what I've gathered, they are in charge of the upper midwest states that border us. He claims his boss is demanding a meeting with you."

Slowly setting my tumbler down, I lean back in my chair and stretch. As I relax, I spot a pile of papers that I forgot all about. Shaking my head, I focus back on David and reply, "I have too much shit to deal with right now, I don't have time for politics. Tell him he is going to have to wait until next week or something." Nodding in understanding, he leaves the office and closes the door behind him.

Returning my attention back to the paper in front of me, I start flipping through it and try to make sense of it all. I don't know how Dominik functioned with how disorganized everything is. I've been going through this office for weeks trying to get everything organized. I think I may have a tad bit of OCD because I've organized his book collection in alphabetical order according to the author's last name, the desk drawers are color-coded and alphabetized, and now, there is a digital copy of every document stored on a secure memory drive. The benefits of being in a relationship with a tech-savvy guy. At the thought of Godfrey, I pull out my phone and shoot a message to him to follow up on his current task.

S: *Hey babe, any update on Neal?*

G: *I keep getting hits off the facial recognition system, but every time one of my guys gets there, he is gone.*

S*: wtf. How is that even possible? It's like he is playing cat and mouse with us.*

G: *I think I may hack my crew's phones. I feel as if we have a snitch in our midst.*

S: *Do what you have to, I want them all out.*

The thought of having a possible mole in

our inner workings sends my blood pressure through the roof. I haven't had an opportunity to hold a meeting with my capos yet, so some of them don't even know who killed Dominik or that he is even dead. I need to get that rectified soon. Going back to my messages, I pull up Frank's thread and start to type a message to him.

Right before I hit send, a knock sounds on the door. Not bothering to look up, I yell, "Come in!"

To my surprise, it's not who I assumed it would be. Instead, it's a brute-looking man walks in with a pissed-off David who has a gun digging into the back of his head. With a shove, David stumbles across the floor and catches himself before he falls. The asshole who barged into my office swings his gun back and forth between David and me. "If either one of ya moves, I'ma fuckin shoot! *Tu me entiende!*"

Rolling my eyes, I let out a sigh and slowly stand from my desk. "I assume you must be Michael."

"My name is nothing to you. I asked for a meeting, and you rudely declined it. So here I am, taking the time I want."

"Well since you waltzed into my office unannounced, I guess you can sit your fat ass down. I have important shit to do, and dealing with you is not one of them." Scowling at my crude comment, he crosses his arms and stays in the doorway. Waving him off, I return to my seat and pull my phone back out. Swiping over to the group message, I send them an alert to come to my office ASAP. "I suggest you either sit down and have this conversation that you couldn't possibly wait for or fucking leave." From the monitors on the wall, I can see my guards rushing up the stairs to get to here.

Snarling at me, the dickwad waves the gun in the air and barks his response. "Ha! I'm the one with the fucking gun, you bitch! Your pathetic guard didn't even have his! So, how about you shut up and listen to what I have to say!" With his gun still in the air, I hide my smirk as one of my guards sneaks up behind him and slams the butt of his gun into the back of dickwad's head. As his weightless body tumbles to the floor, I can't help but smirk. Night-night bitch!

The guards move quickly to secure the gun and cuff the blob on the floor. David ignores them and walks over to me with his fingers flying over his phone. Reaching my desk, he shoves the device into his pocket and lets out a breath. "I'm sorry, Selene, I should have been better prepared. I left my gun in my coat, and he got me while I was coming out of the bathroom. I'll take whatever punishment you deem fit. I already sent a message to Frank and let him know your status."

Propping my elbows on the arms of my chair, I interlock my hands and rest my index fingers against my lips. Now that the immediate threat is neutralized, the cause and effects play back in my mind. When the doors are unlocked, there are always two guards up front, and one in the back. Inside, there should be three scattered around the first floor, and five spread out on the second and third floor at a minimum. Everyone should be armed and wearing their earpieces. No, this isn't all on David. The blame falls on the entire crew. My anger is rapidly reaching the maximum of what I can tolerate before I raise holy fucking hell.

I can feel the heat from my face, and my facial muscles are tight from scowling. David starts to fill the silence, but I raise my hand for him to wait. Raising from my desk, I slowly start to make my way over to the limp body. "Everyone line up. David, retrieve the rest of the guards and lock up the building." No one hesitates to do as I commanded. Maybe it was the no-nonsense tone I have or maybe the expression on my face. Ignoring the buzzing in my back pocket, I squat down and pat the intruder's pockets searching for his wallet.

Finding it quickly in his back pocket, I start to dig through it as I wait for the other guards this buffoon slipped by. I'm hoping to find some usual information, but instead, I find a hotel key card, a wad of cash, a few scribbled on sticky notes, and a picture of what looks to be this dickhead's family. Keeping the wallet in hand, I stand up and walk over to my desk. Tossing the wallet down, I turn and prop myself on the edge of my desk and cross my ankles. My phone hasn't stopped buzzing, and since we are still waiting, I pull it out and see it's Joe calling.

With a swipe of my thumb, I answer the call. "Hello love; you're missing out on my surprise guest." My humor couldn't be any duller. My good vibes are gone, and I just want to fucking strangle someone right about now.

"I heard. We are three minutes out. Who let

the fucker in? Better yet, they are all getting punished." In the background, I can hear Viktor and Frank arguing about something, and knowing Godfrey, he is probably sitting quietly, contemplating revenge.

I watch as the rest of the guards enter my office and step either around or over the body on the floor. They don't meet my eyes and don't question anyone on why they are here. Clicking my tongue, I wrap up my call. "Look, babe, I gotta go. See you in a few, mmkay? Bye!" I don't wait for a response and end the call.

With the phone back in my pocket, I cross my arms and stare at all eleven guards. "So, I'm going to make this short and sweet. Who let him in?" No one responds; instead, they just stare at the floor with their hands clasped behind their back. "No one? Okay, which way did he come in? Let's see if you know that one."

"He had to have come through the back, ma'am. LT and I were at the front and only found out something happened when David came to get us." His tone is so sure and confident, and with a quick glance to LT, he nods his head in agreement.

"Well, that just leaves the back entrance. Because let's be real here gentlemen, that bastard isn't Santa Claus, and we don't have a fucking chimney! Now, I'm going to ask this once. WHO THE FUCK WAS ON THE BACK DOOR?!"

The guard at the end of line steps forward and looks over at me. "I was ma'am. I stepped away to—" I don't let him finish his excuse, the second he stepped forward, I was already in motion. Thankfully the echo of the gun going off wasn't too loud since we are in a well-insulated room. Blood splatter covers the monitors, and the three guards that stood next to him are sprayed with it. The guard standing next to the now-dead guard has a piss spot on the front of his pants and the rest of them all stand unsteadily with their eyes wide.

Michael, the intruder, starts to groan and wiggle on the floor, and I'm guessing he sees the dead body because he starts jerking around and yelling. "What the fuck? This bitch is crazy! Let me go! ¡*El señor de las drogas te atrapa*!" In the middle of his rant, Frank, Viktor, Joe, and Godfrey walk into the office.

Pinching the bridge of my nose, I say whoever is listening, "Can someone knock him out again? I don't want to listen to his shit." I know what *drogas* are. If there is someone who is selling drugs or even calling themselves a drug lord in my territory, we are going to have fucking issues.

The amount of pressure I'm putting on the corner of my eyes is so intense, I can't see out of my eyes, so whoever took the initiative to silence him is in my good graces. Before I can even open my eyes, a warm hand is pulling me into their embrace. Releasing my hand, I blink the spots away and see Godfrey's almond eyes staring down at me. His soft hand glides up my neck and wraps around my neck. Tightening his grip slightly, he raises my chin and meshes his lips with mine.

Our tongues slowly mingle with each other, and our teeth nip at each other's lips. Our movement is languid and sensual. The throbbing in my head is in sync with my heart, but when he pulls away, he releases his grip, and I'm instantly hit with a rush. Leaning forward, I rest my head on his chest and wait for things to return back to normal.

A throat clears, reminding me that I have things that I need to address in the room. Sighing, I step back and turn toward Joe and Frank. "That's the intruder; his name is Michael, and from his outburst, he works for some drug lord. I already checked his wallet, and there was a hotel key in there. Send two of your guys over there to assess what's going on." Looking over to Godfrey, I continue, "Call Jaime, have him run a search on this guy. I want his life history on my desk in forty-eight hours max. I want to know where his kids go to school, who his wife is, and where he's lived in the past ten years. Also, I need you to get information out of him. Use whatever means necessary."

Stepping from the desk, I face the guards and glare at them all. "Every single one of you is on probation until I see fit. You are all a team, so when one fucks up, you all fuck up. So no pay for the next two weeks, you all get dirty jobs, and my guys get to have a solid swing at ya. I want the whole damn facility to know you fucked up. Sporting a black eye shall do it."

They all respond with a "yes ma'am" and brace themselves for the beating they are about to endure. I don't feel like being in the room with a bunch of raging testosterone, so I start making my way out, and as I pass each guy, I steal a desire-fueled kiss from them.

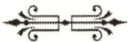

IT DOESN'T take long for the guys to dole out punishments, so by the time they join me at the bar, I'm only finishing up my second shot of tequila. Joe leans beside me and motions over his shoulder. "We are taking this guy down to the basement, there isn't anything down there, and there won't be any curious eyes. Wanna go with us?"

The shot glass in my hands can only hold the answer for little problems, my current headache, unfortunately, is not one of them. Setting it down, I slide from my stool and scowl at the limp body that is being dragged in between Frank and Viktor. "Let's get this shit started. I want to know why he thinks it's perfectly okay to barge into my fucking establishment." The guys only grunt in agreement and start toward the back room where the entrance to the dank basement waits.

I've never been down there in all the years I've worked here, so when they open the door and start their descent, I find myself thoroughly shocked. Instead of a musky, spider-infested area, it is a bright and clean room. The ground is gray concrete, and in the center, there is a drain. Each wall contains some kind of shelving unit and on those shelves are a bunch of tools. At the base of the stairs, there is a rack holding four aprons, and mounted on the wall are boxes of gloves. To top it all off, there is a large steel chair dead center.

As I take in the room, I can't help but whistle my surprise. "Holy shit! What is this? Torture one-oh-one? Remind me to never get on yall's bad side." Behind me, Godfrey's sadistic laugh bounces off the walls, making this room even creepier.

The guys heave Michael into a chair and get him strapped in. I find a spot in the corner to post up and observe. I expect Godfrey to join me on the side, but when I see him again, I can't help but stare. Donned in a thick apron and rubber gloves, he looks as if he is about to butcher the limp person in the chair.

The theory must be readable on my face because the second Godfrey takes in my expression; he curls his lips into a grin more intimidating than the grinch. With that same grin, he walks over one of the walls and removes a hammer, grabs a handful of nails, and pliers off its hook. With everything in hand, he walks over to the intruder and sneers, "Welcome to my hell."

Twelve

A CHILL shoots up my spine and goosebumps cover my arms. Godfrey's icy tone is one I've never heard before, but judging by the expression on the rest of the guys' faces, it's something they've experienced before. I watch as Godfrey circles Michael as if he is prey and Godfrey is looking for a weak spot, a place where he can tackle and destroy his prey without a struggle. Michael finally starts to come to, and as he does, he flinches under the bright light and then looks around. In the brief time he has been awake, I have seen a wider range of emotions than what Frank goes through in an entire day — fear, anger, confusion, and desperation.

Frank, being the lead of security, is the first one to approach the dickwad. "Who sent you here, and what do they want?"

With an audacity he doesn't deserve, dickwad hocks a lo0gie and spits it at Frank. "Fuck you! Each and every one of you are gonna get it, even that dumb cunt over there." The scowl on his face is quickly smacked away by the back of Joe's hand. With the noise-canceling walls, the slap doesn't echo, but I know the bastard will be feeling for a couple of days.

Godfrey's cold glare swings over to me as if he is waiting for me to command him to take retribution. Answering his wordless question, I nonchalantly say, "Y'all can use whatever torture tactics you please. Just keep him alive. I want that fucking idiot to spread the news about who they are trying to fuck with." A sick smile creeps across Godfrey's face as he turns his attention back toward Michael, who is shaking his head as if he doesn't believe shit is going to happen to him.

With every step closer that Godfrey gets, Michael's expression morphs into one of pure terror. He starts squirming in his restraints which makes the chair squeak under his weight. Finding it useless, he starts to yell. His screams are quickly absorbed into the padding of the walls, and when Godfrey is nearly standing on top of him, he quiets down to a whimper.

Godfrey takes the needle nose pliers and advances to the white-knuckled hand that's curling around the arm of the chair. He has to nearly break the dickwad's fingers to get one wrenched off the chair. In a motion quicker than I can follow, Godfrey has an entire nail held up in the air. A shrill scream fills the room as blood starts to drip off the raw flesh. "What the fuck did you do? You're fucking psycho!" Michael's screams are cut off when Joe sucker punches him in the face and nearly knocks him out.

I swear I heard the sound of a bone cracking from the punch that was laid on him. Shaking my head, I continue to watch as Godfrey removes each and every fingernail at a painstakingly slow pace. As the last one falls, Godfrey starts to walk away, and a hoarse Michael sags in relief. Little does he know, this is just the beginning.

Viktor pushes off from his perch and approaches our dim-witted torture participant and slaps him in his upper arm to get his attention. "Who's your boss? Why are you here?" Michael only shakes his head in response. He clams up and locks it all away. Well damn, I'll give him that. He isn't going to break . . . yet.

Pursing his lips, Vik pulls a blade from his pocket and flips it open. The glistening edge of the blade shows how sharp it is, and as he tilts it into the light, it shimmers as if it were made of diamonds. I watch as Vik starts to make slow circles around Michael as if he is debating on which angle he was to approach. On his third lap, he finally puts the blade to the blanched skin. Standing from my chair, I slide my way over to where Joe is standing and lean against him.

From where I'm positioned, I can see the pressure Vik is applying isn't enough to even slice the first layer, but as the cold steel makes contact with Michael's flesh, he jerks and causes the blade to sink into his skin. Unintelligible screams tear from his throat, and he moves some more, only making the wound even worse. Viktor pays no mind to it though; instead, he starts to walk around Michael and drags the blade along with him. Not stopping, he starts to shred the front of Michael's shirt open which leaves a nasty, sweaty, hairy chest exposed.

I nearly gag from how revolting he looks — even worse with all the blood running down his neck and chest. With a scowl, Viktor slams the blade into Michael's thigh and lets it sit there. The movement was done with such force, I could hear the blade scraping against the bone and following right after a scream erupts. Smiling at the pure carnage of what's going on in front of me, I walk over and grip the protruding blade.

My eyes lock with dickwad's bloodshot ones, and I snap at him. "Tell us who your boss is and why the fuck you busted into my establishment!"

"FUCK YOU, YOU CRAZY BITCH!" His face is now bright red, spittle flies out of his mouth, and snot drips out of his nose. His answer doesn't satisfy me, so I twist the blade deeper into his fleshy thigh. Michael's screams fill the room, and the sound of torture gives me a dark sense of satisfaction.

Releasing the blade, I purr out to a retort, "Wanna try that answer again Michael? I'm not the one with a blade shoved in my thigh, surrounded by people who would gladly torture you with a simple command." Through his mangled shouts for mercy, he still managed to curse me to hell and back, and I'm honestly getting fed up with him. My patience for this asshole is wearing thin. But then, the bastard decides he wants to headbutt me.

Without stalling, I yank the dagger out of his thigh all while ignoring the squelching sound as the serrated tip rips through more muscle. Blood starts to ooze out; luckily, it isn't pulsating, so I know his artery is still intact. My head is throbbing from where we made contact, but I push through. Sneering at the bastard, I wave Frank and Godfrey over. "Tilt his head to the side and hold it still." My voice holds such fierce authority that no one questions what I'm going to do or even hesitates. Not that Godfrey would, I mean, from the look in his eyes, he is enjoying this torture to the fullest.

Michael struggles against the hold he is in, which makes Godfrey's muscles bulge. I can't help but drink in his pure fucking sexiness. He has a trim build like a swimmer and all the right muscles to go along with it. Fuck, I really need to get my hands on him. Grunting curses yank me out of the lustful daze I'm in and pull my attention back to the bastard in front of me. Taking a step forward, I reach out and grip the exposed ear that is redder than a fucking fire truck and pull it away from Michael's head. "You have one more fucking chance, or else I'm going to chop your fucking ear off and make you the fucking reincarnation of Van Gogh!" I'm squeezing the handle of the blade so tight it's starting to turn my fingers white, but this bastard is pissing me the fuck off on all kinds of levels.

"I'M NOT TELLING YOU SHIT! FUCKING KILL ME YOU DUMB CUNT!" Michael's fucking call for death makes me itch to make it happen, but I need to pass a message to his boss. So, no one is dying today.

My head falls back as I let out an exasperated groan, "Fine, you obviously don't fucking listen." With a flick of my wrist, I slice his ear off and watch as blood starts gushing from the open wound. With the fatty cartilage in hand, I take the opportunity to shove it in his gaping mouth as he screams bloody murder. Shaking his head, he tries to fling the chunk of his ear out of his mouth. Gagging noises sound in between the screams and his voice cracks as if it is nearly gone. Turning away from Michael, I stride toward Godfrey and wrap my bloodied hand around his neck and pull him down.

Our lips meet with a bruising force, but I don't fucking care. I love the pain that his eyes promise me, and with the way he grips my waist, I know that whatever he throws my way will be painfully amazing. Sucking on his bottom lip, I give it a nip and moan as the taste of iron explodes in my mouth. Godfrey's grip on my waist tightens, and his nails bite into my skin through my shirt. Let there be bruises; I'll proudly show them to the fucking world. Sliding closer to him, I press my body against his trim frame and gasp when I feel his rigid cock pressing against my belly.

Pulling back from my venturing mouth, Godfrey lets out a frustrated groan and rests his hands on my shoulders to hold me back. "As much as I would like to take this further, Blue, we need to get him out of here before we have a dead body in your establishment." With a pout, I turn my attention over to Michael, who is silently sobbing and reaching for whatever is left of his ear while the cut off chunk lays on the floor in between his feet.

"Fine, guys, let's get him out of here and deliver him to his house. Once you get him out of our hands, come home to me." My need is laced in my command, and from the sultry looks Frank, Joe, and Viktor are giving me, they heard it. Looking down at myself, I scowl at the blood covering me and start to wipe my hands off. A snort escapes me as the blood only smears further on my hands and now more so on my clothes. Rolling my eyes, I hand Godfrey the knife that I'm still holding and make my way over to the stairs. "I'll be at the apartment. I'm starving, and I want that fucker's blood off of me."

They all grunt in understanding and without waiting any longer, I climbed the stairs and exited out of the torture chamber. As I emerge, I notice the halls are fuller than when we went down, and nearly everyone turns their head. Thank fuck everyone knows better than to question why I look like Carrie, so I make it out the back exit without any hassle. Jumping into my truck, I jam the key into the ignition, turn my monster on, and speed out of there.

I'm only two blocks away before my cell starts vibrating in my pocket and with it paired to the Bluetooth in my truck, I notice it's Mr. Devoy, the Director of the FBI. What on god's earth is he doing calling me? Pursing my lips, I press the answer button on my steering wheel. "What do I owe the pleasure, old man?"

The sound of his phone being lifted from the receiver sounds followed by a cough to clear his throat. "I wanted to let you know I just intercepted a call to the police. There was a civilian calling frantic saying she saw a woman with bright blue hair covered in blood. You wouldn't happen to know who that is, would you Selene?"

Cursing under my breath, I make a mental note to ask Viktor to watch the security cameras to check who the snitch was. "I wouldn't have a single clue. You know I'm not the only one with blue hair so it's kinda presumptuous that you would instantly think of me."

"This may be true, but you are the only one who happens to work at Sub Rosa. Is that not the truth?" His snarky comment makes my blood start to boil. With him on my payroll, I have no worries about things getting out of control. Little slip ups like that usually get brushed under the rug, and the fact he thinks he can intimidate me makes me want to drag him down to the fucking torture room.

The car in front of me slams on their breaks which causes a chain reaction, so I lay on my horn. When the noise is gone, I snap back a retort, "Cut the shit Devoy; you know that call will end up nowhere. What's the real fucking reason you called?" There's always a fucking reason when people call with stupid shit.

Devoy releases a deep sigh, and after a few seconds, he replies in a quiet voice as if he doesn't want anyone else to hear. "There has been a development in Dominik's case that I need to discuss with you. It's rather urgent, so if you can come by the office, I would appreciate it." His sincere tone is shocking to me considering the fact he was just being a dick.

Gripping the steering wheel, I look down at myself and check the time. It's just after five, and by the time I get showered and over to the department, it would be around seven. "Today isn't good, let me know the next time you'll be in the office, and I'll swing by."

"Will do. Stay safe Selene, and for crying out loud, try not to create chaos." With a laugh, I hang up on him and continue my drive to the apartment with Breaking Benjamin blaring through my speakers. Thankfully, the streetlights are all in my favor, and I somehow beat the afternoon rush, so I make it to our apartment a lot quicker than I anticipated.

With my truck parked safely in the corner, I sneak my way through the apartment building and climb into the elevator. Pulling out the key that lets me override the elevator, I make the elevator skip all floors but mine. I don't like using the damn thing, but there's no way in hell I can let the rest of the residents who would have climbed on, see me like this. When I reach my floor, I turn the override off, climb out and head straight toward the guys' apartment. As I walk through their front door, all their manly smells fill me and a sense of home courses through me. With trudging steps, I make my way to Joe's room, steal an oversized T-shirt, and go to their shared master bathroom.

These men of mine make sure I have my own supplies here, so when I emerge from my invigorating shower, I smell like the sweetest vanilla. The hot shower must have relaxed me more than I imagined because by the time I have the shirt on, I'm ready to pass out. Exiting the bathroom, I turn toward the left and enter Godfrey's room. Crisp white sheets and an oversized downy comforter call my name, so with sluggish steps, I answer the call. Falling on his king-size mattress, I crawl to the center and wrap myself up.

Thirteen

FUCK, MY bladder is killing me. I try to roll out of bed, but a strong arm is draped over my waist and is holding me down. Carefully lifting it up, I somehow maneuver out of Godfrey's hold and scoot to the edge of the bed. A gush of wetness floods my lady bits, and the realization hits me: I started my fucking period. Jumping up, I shuffle to the bathroom and plop down on the cold toilet seat. Dread fills me as I take in the bloody massacre that's running down my thighs. I didn't put any underwear on after my shower, so nothing was stopping the blood from running.

After a quick clean up, I tiptoe back into the bedroom and freeze when I see Godfrey awake and removing his now blood-stained sheets. My heart seizes up in my chest, and my cheeks burn with embarrassment. "I'm so sorry, babe; I didn't know it was going to start! I'm on depo, so I stopped having them over six months ago!" I frantically get my words out to explain myself, but as they spill out, Godfrey stills.

With a confused expression, he drops the ruined sheets and approaches me. Reaching up, Godfrey cradles my face in between his hands as if I'm a delicate flower that could fall apart with the slightest movement. "It's okay. I can wash them, and if anything, I can get new ones. I can honestly care less about them. However, I want you to go hop in the shower and get cleaned up. We will get your supplies, and once you are ready, we are going to go back to my bed and sleep. Is that understood?" Dominance exudes from him, yet his facial expression is nothing but understanding.

I have to fight myself from questioning him. I know he needs control and everything about him makes me want to trust that he will take care of me, no matter the situation. With a quick peck to his cheek, I turn on my heels and reenter the bathroom. Looking down at myself, I see blood is running down my thighs, and it's nearly past my knees. Shaking my head, I make a mental note to check the date I got my last birth control injection.

Halfway through the shower, I feel the weight of lack of sleep bearing down on me. Closing my eyes, I lose myself in the soothing heat that soaks deep into me and relaxes my body so much that I'm nearly mush. The feeling of an arm wrapping around me from behind causes me to jump and scream damn near bloody murder. While screaming, I involuntarily jab my elbow back, causing an oomph to escape whoever is behind me. Spinning in his arms, I take in who is behind me. Standing with a cocky grin and in nothing but what he was born in, is Joe.

Tucking my bottom lip between my teeth, I slowly take in his delectable form and pause as my eyes land on his dick that is jutting out from his pelvis. With such little space between us, his gorgeous member bobs less than an inch from the top of my slit. Inwardly cursing myself, I remember why I'm in the shower in the first place. Groaning in disappointment, I shake my head and place both my hands on his chest to push him away. "I'm sorry, babe, as much as I want your dick, I can't."

When I start to push him out of the shower, he reaches up and grasps my wrists which interlocks them together. To free one of his hands, he wraps his fingers around both my wrists and twirls me back around so that my ass now cradles his solid cock. With his free hand now on my hip, he pulls me closer to him and leans down, so his mouth is next to my ear and whispers, "I'm a real man, princess, blood won't stop me from burying myself inside you."

As the last word passes his lips, he descends and starts to leave a trail of smoldering kisses from behind my ear, down my neck, and stopping at the dip in my collar bone. Darting his tongue out, he laps the water that pools there and then starts his way back up again. Lost in the feeling of his soft lips caressing my skin, I loll my head to the side and slowly start to grind myself against his nestled dick.

Arching my back, I lay my head against his shoulder. This change in positions puts my pert nipples in line with the high water pressure that is streaming from the showerhead. The jet-like stream bites into my skin and sends perfectly painful sensations straight down to my core. Biting back a moan, I swivel my hips and grind back against Joe's lengthy member. His grip on my hip tightens and stills my movements.

"I told you a little blood doesn't bother me, princess, now spread those legs and put both your hands on the wall." Joe's husky voice knocks away all my doubt, and without any further thought, I do as he says. With slow movements, I get into the position he wants and look over my shoulder. His eyes are locked on my ass, and from the way my back is arched, he is probably getting an eye full of my pussy as well. The look of pure desire fills his expression and seeing that makes me clench with need.

With his gaze still on my parted pussy lips, he grips my hip with one hand and uses the other to guide his dick inside of me. "Yesss." My moan drags out as every inch slides deeper into me. He stills to give my channel a chance to stretch around his delicious girth, but fuck with my hormones going crazy, I don't want to wait, so instead, I shove the rest of him inside me with one push. "God, you're so fucking big Joseph!"

Now fully seated inside of me, I wait for him to start fucking me, but to my dismay, he just laughs and snorts. "So I'm Joseph now, when did this start?"

"Joe, Joseph, Tomato, Tamahto. Same thing. Now, fuck me!" To egg him on, I start to fuck him myself, in slow torturous thrusts. He doesn't stop me; instead, he digs his fingers into my hips and lets out a groan of approval. The vibration that comes from his chest travels down his body right to his dick that's buried inside of me. All my nerves are overly sensitive so that extra sensation causes a flood, of what, I don't want to fucking know.

Joe releases my hips from his bruising grip, drags his hands up my back, and swipes my drenched turquoise hair out of the way. Gripping both of my shoulders, he starts to slam into me with punishing thrusts. With the walls and water amplifying all the sounds coming from us, I'm sure everyone in the apartment knows we are fucking. The thought of that makes me even hotter and adds to the fire burning inside of me.

Pleasure licks at my core and I start to tremble as the inferno engulfs me. I can barely hold myself up, so I dig my nails into the grout between the tiles. My feet start to slide further apart, which only gives Joe more room to slam his pelvis closer. With each thrust, I come closer and closer to exploding. His thrusts start to lose rhythm and signals he's about to come. The urge to finish with him has me moving my hand down my body and straight to my swollen nub. I buck as I start to rub fast circles, each lap syncing up with each thrust.

"Come, baby, come with me, squeeze my cock with your fucking pussy!" Joe's straining voice spurs me on and with a few more swirls and a pinch, I detonate. My eyes squeeze shut, and white lights illuminate the back of my lids. Joe muffles my scream of pleasure as he leans over and captures my mouth. He continues to pump into me and drags my orgasm out, but after our mouths connect, he stills with one last grunt into my mouth. Ropes of his scorching cum fill me, coating me completely.

With a nip to his lip, I pull back and drag a ragged breath in. Joe drops his head to my shoulder as he slows his breathing down, and with the slowest movement, he withdraws from me. Looking down at him, I notice his dick is covered in not only his cum and my juices but proof of my period. I inwardly start to panic at the amount of it and brace for Joe's reaction. Straightening up, I step to the side and allow water to cascade over him.

Joe reaches out and tilts my chin, so I'm looking him in the eyes. "I love you, princess, all of you. Even this. This right here just lets me know that once a day, I might be able to have a baby inside of you." My eyes fly open, and my eyebrows raise so far up, I swear they are off my face. I wait for his usual joking personality, but everything about Joe is sincere.

After a few seconds, I melt into his hand and close the distance between us. Raising up on my toes, I plant a quick, yet passionate kiss on his lips and whisper, "I love you too Joe, forever and always."

With a smile, he responds, "And a day, my queen." With one last kiss, we clean up and hop out of the shower.

Sitting on the counter is everything I need to go back to bed without any more messes. Once dressed again, I part ways with Joe and enter Godfrey's room. Laying in bed is my dark ninja, staring at me as if I'm his prey. Lifting the blankets, he pats the spot beside him, motioning for me to join him. Sauntering over, I climb onto the bed and make my way to his waiting arms. Lying on my side, I drape my leg over his and wrap my arm over his chest. With his bicep being used as my pillow, I snuggle close to him and let sleep claim me once again.

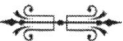

THE SECOND time I wake up, it's to the smell of bacon. The bed is empty next to me; however, on the nightstand sits a bottle of water and a pill. Below that is a note.

Good morning, Blue, take this ibuprofen and drink some water. Take care of yourself, eat some breakfast, and rule the world.

Snorting at the note, I shake my head and take the medication. Another waft of bacon aroma fills my senses and makes my stomach growl, so without putting it off any more, I slide out of bed and make my way to the bathroom. After a quick clean up, I make my way to the kitchen and prop myself up against the wall to take in the scene in front of me. Dressed in nothing but plaid pajama pants and an apron is Viktor, who is dancing around the kitchen, and flipping bacon. I have no clue what he is listening to, but when he turns his head, I catch the white of his ear pods.

My hand covers the laugh that bubbles out of me, but my body starts to shake at all the ridiculous moves he starts busting out. Walking over, I wrap my arms around his waist, which causes him to startle. Unable to control myself anymore, I let out a full belly laugh. Viktor sets the spatula down, removes his ear pods, and then wraps me into his arms. Together we laugh like our lives depend on it and nearly fall to the ground in hysterics.

After a few minutes of wheezing from laughing so hard, Viktor releases me from his embrace and gives me a good-morning kiss. Returning back to the nearly burnt food, he quickly removes everything from the stove and starts to make our plates. While he does that, I set the table and grab our drinks. This morning routine feels so right and normal, I never thought I would see myself in this kind of situation, but fuck, I'm grateful to have them in my life.

With everything set, we both sit down and start to dig in. Looking up from my plate, I realize that Viktor and I are the only ones at the table. Shit, where has my mind been all day? Swallowing the food that I'm chewing on, I look over to Vik and ask, "Where is everyone else?"

Taking a swig of his juice, he clears his throat and replies, "Godfrey had to play babysitter for some senator, Frank is still dealing with the security issue, Joe is over at the apartments where the girls stay because of some catfight, and Jaime, well I don't know where he is. He slipped out of the house before anyone got up." His brows furrow as if in deep thought, but his vibrating phone drags him back to reality. Glancing at his phone, he scans the message and then looks back at me, "Want to go with me to visit Dominik's gravesite?"

My lips curl in a pout, I haven't been to visit

Dominik since the funeral, and the sheer thought of being there brings a looming cloud over me. A piece of my heart chips away as I remember all the good times we had together, but I know visiting him is something I need to do. I roll my neck to relieve the tension, and with an unsure tone, I reply, "Sure, I mean, of course. Let's finish breakfast first. I'll text David and have him push my meetings back."

"No need, that was Frank, he said he already handled your meetings for today, and he wants you to take the day off." Waving away my concern, he turns back to his plate and continues to eat his breakfast. Looking down at my plate, I fumble with the idea of taking the day off. I could stop by and see Octavia after the cemetery. Hell, maybe take her out for lunch or something. Letting out a resigned sigh, I shake my head and then finish my breakfast.

Once we finish, we quickly clean the kitchen and get ready for today. Back over at my apartment, I slip on a pair of skinny jeans, an off-the-shoulder tee, and my black Vans. With a quick spritz of perfume, a swipe of eyeliner, and a messy bun, I am ready to go. By the time I exit my bedroom, Vik is leaning against my counter and scrolling through his phone. Looking up from his device, he slowly scans my body, and when our eyes meet, he winks. Shooting him a quick smirk, I walk over to the door and call out, "You coming or what?" With a snort, he pushes off the counter and follows me out of the door and into the waiting elevator.

Fourteen

OUR RIDE to the cemetery is filled with the soothing sounds created from Bach, Mozart, and Beethoven. I would have never thought Viktor, my leather-and-stud-clad man, would listen to classical music. But the way he taps his fingers and hums along shows me he legitimately enjoys it. Leaning back in my seat, I pull out my phone and tap into the dark web. Godfrey and I have been taking turns searching through it ever since Dominik was murdered; however, our search hasn't yielded anything yet.

Even today's search didn't pull anything up. Well, except for a couple calls for hits or orders for back-alley deals. Forwarding those messages to the rest of the guys, I exit the dark web and tuck my phone away. Turning my attention out the window, I take in the cemetery that is looming ahead of us. The wrought iron fence and brickwork look weathered and tarnished from all the harsh weather that has passed through the years, but as we drive past the metal archway, the handiwork of the grave keeper comes into view. The grass is manicured, and every vase holds fresh flowers, there are no overgrown weeds, and nearly every tombstone is shining as if it was recently cleaned.

I glance over to Viktor to see if he is seeing what I'm seeing. I've slept in plenty of graveyards before when I lived on the street, but never have I seen one this nice. "I guess the groundskeeper has put our donations to good use." My voice shows the awe that I'm in. Appreciation for the man caring for those laid to rest here flows through me.

Viktor gives me a crooked grin and says, "He has put every dime into this cemetery. Instead of taking care of himself, he hired some veterans to lighten the load and spread the care to the whole field."

Closing my gaping mouth, I snort at the old man's generosity. "Well, give him a bonus. Add the stipulation that he has to use this money for himself on shoes and clothes. If we have to take him ourselves, we will. He is taking care of the man I call father, so he gets respect from the family."

As we pull up to the curb next to the path that leads to Dominik's resting spot, Vik nods his head in agreement and sends a quick text to whomever. With the SUV in park, I hop out and start the trudge up the small hill to Dom's burial site. As I approach, my steps slow, and I feel the sadness that I locked away pressing to get out. With a gulp, I close the distance and stand to the side of his grave. Resting my hand on the cool granite, I drop my chin and tuck my bottom lip in between my teeth. Tears start to cloud my vision, so I take a deep breath and blink them away.

With my vision now clear, I finally notice the vase and the vibrant red roses that fill it. Squatting down, I run my finger over the velvety petals and get lost in my thoughts. A couple of minutes later, the sound of someone approaching shakes me out of my stupor. Looking over my shoulder, I realize it's Vik approaching so I stand up and hold my hand out to him. Clasping my hand, he pulls me to his side and wraps his arms around my waist. Looking up at him, I ask a question that has been festering in my mind. "Do you think he is proud of me? I mean, with the business and well, everything else?"

With a kiss to the top of my head, he responds, "The business is thriving, there hasn't been any attacks or call to arms. We have expanded our reach, and Club Rosa is at an increase. Everyone wants to see Dominik Romanov's prodigy. You may not be as active as you want to be, but that's because your men are handling it for you. Dominik delegated duties to us before he was murdered and we haven't stopped since. In the end, all decisions are yours. So yes, I think Dominik would be proud of you." Each word he speaks wipes away lingering doubt and shines a light on the tasks I have been performing. With a renewing breath, I look down to Dom's resting spot and blow him a kiss.

Movement to my right catches my eye, flickering my attention toward the disturbance, and I spot the caretaker. Patting Vik's hand to let me go, I start my way over. The small trek over to him gives me the chance to observe the headstones that I pass and allows me to take note of their names and the unique epitaphs. Though I don't know any of them, I still respect them and avoid walking on their graves. After careful maneuvering, I finally make it over and stop behind the headstone of the grave the groundskeeper is currently working on.

Tucking my hands into my back pockets, I rock on the balls of my feet and wait for the groundskeeper to finish what he is doing. Looking around, I see a car pull in, and an elderly couple emerges. Looking away from them, I turn my focus back on the tired man in front of me. "I like what you did to the place. I don't think I've ever since a cemetery look this inviting. Oh, by the way, I never did get your name."

Lifting his floppy hat to the side, he peers up to me, stops pulling weeds, and brushes his hands off on his pants. Clearing his parched throat, he responds, "I'm sorry about that ma'am. My name is Albert, but everyone calls me Al." After a quick check of his hand, he extends it out to me. I pay no mind to the dirt that clings to his hands or the grime under his nails. The filth doesn't make me cringe, hell, it makes me respect him more.

Giving his hand a squeeze, I let go of it and watch as he winces as he notices the smudges on my pale skin. Not bothering to wipe it off, I say, "Well, Al, it's nice to meet you officially and on better terms. Oh, speaking of, thank you for keeping Dominik's burial neat and proper." Al's already wrinkled complexion crinkles even more at the mention of Dom, his smile turns into a frown, and his yellow-tinged eyes dart down as if to hide the sadness.

Walking around the stone, I approach his side and drop down to my knees with my feet tucked beneath me. Reaching out, I start pulling the weeds that he hasn't gotten a chance to get to. Albert doesn't say anything; instead, he gives me a raised eyebrow and picks up where he left off. We don't say much as we pull the weeds together, he does, however, tell me how to properly pull the weeds out, which apparently means digging your fingers into the soil to grasp the root. A few more mumbled words, and we finish weeding the area. With all the rubbish picked up and thrown away, I stand from the ground and spot Viktor making his way over. When he is finally near us, he nods his head in greeting to Albert and then looks to me. "What's going on over here?"

Giving him a quick once over, I notice the redness that still lingers in his eyes, not wanting to broach the topic, I wave down to the grave and respond, "Albert and I just finished removing the weeds from . . ." Glancing down, I read the headstone and freeze. My brain ceases as I take in the name of the person lying six feet deep. "Jelena Romanov, Daughter of Dominik Romanov. My gaze darts over to Viktor, searching for an explanation, but he looks just as shocked as me. Instead, I turn my attention to Albert as if the groundskeeper would have any information. Pointing down to the headstone, I grind out my command, "What is this, Albert?

Did . . . did Dominik have a secret daughter?"

Raising his hands as if to show innocence, he just shakes his head and pinches his mouth shut. Anger flashes through Viktor, causing to stomp over to Albert and jab him in the shoulder with his finger. "Who the fuck is that groundskeeper? Tell us what you know!" With another shove, Albert stumbles, and falls to the ground. His frail body rattles from the impact, but he keeps his wallows to himself.

If anything hurt him, he didn't let it show; instead, he slowly rights himself and utters, "I'm not sure, sir, I was just doing my job. I may talk to the dead, but they never respond." Crackles fill his voice and sympathy for the old man fills me. Holding a hand out to him, I assist him back to a standing position and cross my arms over my chest.

Agitation makes me bristle, and I start to shuffle from one foot to another. I flick my eyes back and forth from Viktor to Albert, and finally, when the silence couldn't get any more uncomfortable, I shoot Albert a tense smile and say, "If you can think of anything, give me a call. Oh and Albert, take care of yourself." The disheveled old man nods his head and gives Viktor and me a mock salute before we depart from him.

After dodging the gravesites, we finally end up back on the trail, so with a clear path to the SUV, we intertwine our fingers and let the crunch of dead leaves fill the silence between us. Back in the passenger seat, I pull out my phone and shoot a message to Octavia.

S: *How are you feeling bestie?*

O: *Fucking pissy, I want out of this house, the damn guard dogs you got watching the place won't let me.*

S: *Well you're in luck, Viktor and I are on the way to get you, so get your ass dressed. xoxo*

O: *About fucking time you punta!*

Smiling down at her message, I shake my head at her usual snarky comment. Fuck, I missed my best friend. With my phone now locked and residing on the center console, I reach over and grasp Vik's hand. "Let's go get my best friend. I hope you're up for a day of shopping." I can't help but let the humor and excitement filling me spill out, and it must be contagious because a jovial grin forms on Vik's face.

Giving my hand a squeeze, he looks over at me and snarkily retorts, "Until midnight tonight, your wish is your command, my queen. That was Frank's order, and I am more than willing to oblige." Lifting my hand, he brings it to his lips and places a chaste kiss on it. With a final squeeze, he turns back to the road and drives us to our next destination.

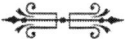

FOUR HOURS, two pretzels, and a couple hundred dollars later, we finally make it back to my apartment. Our outing was full of laughs and consisted of one less body since the last time I went out. Even with all underground business pushed to the side, I still have the site of the gravestone lingering right in the forefront. Pursing my lips together, I debate about how I should handle the situation. I start to mindlessly scroll through my phone and freeze when I pass two names who might know: Doris and Doyle.

My fingers glide over the luminescent screen as I type out my request to speak with both of them, along with adding onto Doris's message that I still have something for her from when the will was reviewed. Luckily, they both respond quickly and agree to the times I requested. With there being nothing else that I can do, I try to ignore the thoughts and refocus on what's going on around me. Scanning the apartment, I see Tavia holding up a new dress to her chest and talking animatedly to Frank, Joe, and Viktor, all while Godfrey and Jaime are nowhere to be seen. Now that I think about it, I actually haven't heard from Jaime all day.

Standing from the comfy-as-fuck recliner that I have claimed, I start my way over to join in with Tavia's conversation. As I walk over, I give Jaime a call to check up on him, but after a few rings, I go to voicemail. Frowning down at my phone, I hang up without leaving a message and right before I can send him a text, Octavia calls out, "Selene! Tell them how fucking awesome it is for this dress to have pockets!" To emphasize her flamboyancy, she holds the dress up against her chest with one arm, slides her free hand into the said pockets, and sash stays in a circle.

Closing the distance, I grasp at the cotton material and inspect it further. "Well shit, I didn't realize it had pockets! That's so cute!" Sliding my hand into the open pocket, I gasp at how deep it is. "Well shit, this is fucking amazing, I can fit nearly everything in there! I'm going to have to borrow this dress, better yet, I'm just going to order my own!" Looking over toward my guys, I notice they are all staring at us with looks of bewilderment, amusement, and confusion. Shaking my head, I wave them off and turn back toward Tavia and say, "Psh, men, they will never understand."

With a click of her tongue, Tavia throws the dress over her arm and motions for me to follow her. "Come on, chica; let's put these away while they order food. I'm starving." After giving the guys our order for lunch, we grab our bags and head over to my apartment.

I'm nearly done putting all my purchases away when I peek over to glance over to Tavia and see her looking down at her hands that are resting in her lap. Darkness now overshadows her previously bright expression. With my eyes locked on her, I hastily hang up the shirt that's in my hands and then walk over to where she is sitting. She's so lost in her thoughts that she doesn't notice me sitting next to her. The moment my hand makes contact with her shoulder, she jumps and looks to me with her eyes blinking as if in shock. Keeping my voice low, I utter, "Are you okay, love? What's going on?"

After a few seconds of picking at her jeans, she lets out a deep, sorrowful sigh and leans against me. With her head tucked underneath my chin, I wrap her in my arms and slowly start to rock her. When her body starts to shake from the silent sobs, I coo to her that things are going to be alright and that I'm there for her. I have no idea what's going on, but I have a feeling this is something that has to do with Neal. My best friend is scared of him just as much as I am, hell if not more. She was sleeping with the enemy and couldn't do anything about it.

I don't pressure her to talk to me or even to stop crying; instead, I continue to hold my best friend. The one woman who has always been there for me, through rain and shine. She trained me when I was a server, helped me ace mixing drinks, and taught me how to suck a dick properly without gagging. There are no limits for the amount of love I have for her, and I know she feels the same. The simmering anger of what happened to her and Dominik flares like a raging inferno, a newfound desire to make Neal pay is all I can think about.

As a whimper escapes Tavia, I run my hand over her head in a soothing manner. That newfound desire resonates a silent promise to my best friend. I will not only get revenge for Dominik, but I will get it for her. I will eliminate the cause of her sorrows, and I don't give a fuck who plans on stopping me. I'm the fucking boss!

Fifteen

IT'S BEEN three days since Octavia's breakdown. After nearly an hour of her crying, she finally opened up and confirmed my suspicions. She's been having nightmares that Neal comes back and takes over, that he ends up killing not only my guys but me as well. As she spilled her nightmares, chills overtook my body, the hair on the back of my neck stood at full attention, and my jaw ticked from the amount of pressure I was applying when as I clenched it. Since that day, I doubled my efforts in finding Neal. As part of those efforts, I increased the bounty for whoever turns him into to me, dead or alive. I think fifty thousand should light a fire under their asses.

  Reports of sightings have increased, along with more helpful information. Unfortunately, the extra heat to find him leads to increased violence. Two of my own are in the ICU after a drive-by gone bad. Got the fucking attention of Mr. Devoy. That fucker was tucked nicely in his office, and then boom, some petty shit happens and now he has to show his aging face. Thank fuck my lackeys have some kind of brains and that Doyle, our lawyer, knows how to work the system because once they heal, those fuckers are getting out scot-free.

Pushing out a deep breath, I sign the last check made out to the hospital for their care of my lackeys and then slide it into the designated envelope. I've spent nearly all day in meetings and reviewing the job contracts that have been submitted. Thank fuck, I only have one more left. Bonus points it's at an upscale restaurant because I've only had a chance to down two granola bars. After a quick check of the time, I close down my computer, grab my phone and purse, and then head to the destination.

On the way there, I shoot a group text to my guys letting them know where I'll be, and of course, they all get pissy because I'm not bringing one of them with me. To calm them down, I turn on my location that's built into my phone and promise to carry my handgun with me. They send a couple more disgruntled texts, but finally concede and continue with their own business. The restaurant that the meeting is being held at is only about twenty minutes from the club, but with the traffic working in my favor, I get there in fifteen. Handing my keys to the valet, I head into the building and nearly stumble with how dark it is.

Everything about this petite restaurant is quaint and exudes a sense of secrecy or even romance. With a quirked eyebrow, I walk up to the receptionist, inform her of the code name that the reservation is under, and follow her to our table. As I pass multiple tables, I start to take in the decorations and become aware of the other people around me. Every table is covered in black lace or silk, silver candelabras hold black candles, and rose vines look as if they are climbing the back wall that leads into the kitchen.

The receptionist stops at a large curved table in the back corner, hidden away from prying eyes and turns to me. "This is the table that was requested, please have a seat, and when your other guest arrives, I'll bring him back." Nodding my head, I climb into the bench and slide to the point that allows me a view of all doors and will allow me to have quick access to the exit. Pulling my phone out, I let my guys know I made it and check the time. Only five more minutes until the scheduled time, he has ten minutes, and if no one shows, I'm out.

I'm only left alone for a few minutes until the waiter approaches the table with a bottle of wine in hand. In the dark lighting, from what I can tell, he looks like he is barely eighteen. Stopping in front of my table, he bows to me in greeting and then shoots me a grin. "Good evening, ma'am, can I interest you in some wine? Complimentary, of course." Fuck, for someone who looks so young he has a deep voice. Not to mention he is laying the flirting on pretty thick; husky voice and winking all at the same time.

I'm going to blame the atmosphere, but his little flirting just made me blush. Gesturing to the wine glass, I answer him. "Well, if you insist. I'm not much of a wine drinker, but what the hell, it's on the house." The server gives me what has to be his million-dollar smile and then fills my glass, so it's over half full. As I take the glass from him, his fingers linger and then slide against mine as he pulls away. Bringing the glass to my lips, I hide the chuckles that I can't help but let out. If only he knew who he is messing with and how many men await me at home.

He waits for me to take a sip of the wine, and once I hum in approval, he walks away. I spend the rest of my time sipping the wine and watching the people that come and go from the restaurant. Checking the time, I see that it's been nine minutes, so I down the rest of the wine and start to slide out. As I'm looking down to make sure I clear the legs of the table, someone slams their hand on the tabletop and startles me. My hand goes to my concealed gun, and I start to pull it out. Looking up, I glare at the cause. Standing in front of me is a heavy-set man dressed in a grey tweed suit that looks like it's nearly bursting at the seams. Almost like a busted can of rolls.

"I didn't realize Dominik was that foolish, but when he designated you as the prodigy, I nearly laughed at the joke. But I guess he was that dumb." A sneer fills his fat face, and as his eyes trail over me, the sneer only deepens. With his eyes locked on me, he pulls out a cigar and places it between his wrinkled lips. Patting around his coat, he hunts for a lighter but comes up short. Looking around, he spots the candle on our table and uses that instead. My eyebrows nearly fly off my face at what he's doing and the fact he is smoking inside the restaurant when they clearly don't allow it inside the building.

Shaking my head, I slide back onto the bench, but this time, closer to the edge. I don't know who this is or what he wants, but I need to make sure all my options are available. I watch him struggle to get his cigar lit, and when he does, he takes a deep inhale and then sits on the opposite side of the table from me. I expect him to be a dick and blow his smoke at me, but instead, he releases it in a plume above us. My eyes dart toward the waiter and then to the receptionist, both shooting him scowls, yet they look scared at the same time. Interesting.

Straightening myself up, I look to him and start to dig at the reason we are here. "So, who are you and what's the reason for this meeting? Let's not play games either, you showed up nearly five minutes late, and I have shit to do. So, out with it." I cross my arms to emphasize my annoyance, and with the way I spit my words out to him, he should realize that I'm being fucking serious.

Leaning back against the bench, he pulls the cigar from lips and stares at it as he twirls it between his fat fingers. Without looking at me, he grunts and replies, "I'm surprised you don't know who I am, but since you're a female and your position is not here at this table, I'll tell you. My name is Giovanni Moretti, the Don of everything south of your inherited line. What I'm doing here sounds better now that I met you." With his free hand, he starts to stroke his unkempt beard and then turns to me. "I'm going to make you an offer, and you're going to accept it, capisce?"

Surprised by his sheer audacity, I lean back and fight to hold in a laugh. It seems I have a misogynistic bastard on my hands. With my lips pursed, I run my hands down the soft denim of my jeans and click my tongue against the roof of my mouth. "Is that so? Here's the thing, Giovanni, I do what the fuck I want to do, when the fuck I want to, and how the fuck I want to. So, you making the assumption that I will willingly agree is quite absurd if you ask me."

Spitting to the side, Giovanni snarls at me and points at me with the hand that holds the wobbling cigar. "Listen here you little cunt, I'm going to give you fifty thousand, and you are going to pack your shit and leave fucking town. Better yet, leave the country. I'm done with the niceties. I got your little fucking message that you left me by leaving my capo at death's door. So, I'm giving you two weeks to pack up and leave. End of story!" With spittle flying out of his mouth, he jumps up from the bench which makes his gut nearly tip the table over. Letting out an enraged grunt, he slides out the rest of the way and storms out of the building.

My trigger finger itches to be used but with all the attention I'm getting right now, I know it wouldn't be worth it. Looking back at the disheveled table, I notice my glass of wine is still intact. I barely have the chance to get my hand wrapped around the stem before my waiter starts speed walking over to me. His eyes are as wide as saucers, his mouth is gaping like a fish, and his words come out in a stutter. "I'm s-s-sorry, ple-e-ase let me straighten t-t-his up p-p-please m-ma'am. P-please don't-t report m-e-e to the b-o-ss."

His hands are trembling so bad he can barely pick up the scattered silverware and what he just said doesn't make sense. Confusion overtakes me and his shaky movement starts to become annoying so throwing my hand out, I grab his wrist and make him freeze. Glaring up to him, I see his eyes darting from where my hands grips his wrist to the front of the restaurant where a man in a sleek suit now stands. In a barely audible whisper, I pry, "Why would I report you to your boss? Better yet, who is your boss?"

"Mr. R-Romano-v-v owns the restaurant, but his n-n-ephew is our boss. He said to make sure you're n-not bothered."

Ah, well poor boy doesn't know the change in command and probably doesn't know what happened. With his wrist free of my grip, I slide out of the booth and straighten my outfit out. My eyes lock on the man standing at the front of the restaurant, and without looking away, I soothe the waiter's worries. "I'm not sure what you know, but Dominik Romanov is dead. All his business have been passed to me, and that nephew you speak of is Viktor. He is my . . . partner if you will." Pulling out my wallet from my purse, I slide out a couple of twenties and toss them on the table. "Don't stress out, kid, I'm a big girl, and I can handle myself."

With a reassuring pat on his back, I walk past him and head toward the man who has yet to take his eyes off of me. With the shadows hiding most of his features, it's hard to tell who it is or if I even know him. As I reach the middle of the restaurant, my eyes finally adjust, and I realize it's Frank. His intense gaze stays on me, even when I'm standing toe to toe with him. But as I stand on my tippy-toes, Frank softens up and wraps me in his arms.

Looking up at him, I catch the love he has for me showing. Frank generally doesn't show his emotions out in public. He saves those times for me at home, in bed. So seeing it here makes me want to melt against him even more, but with what I just went through, my swooning has to wait. Stretching the rest of the way, I place a chaste kiss on his slightly-parted lips and then turn to exit the restaurant.

WHEN WE have all gathered around in the living room of our apartment, I tell the guys what went down. They all yell questions at once, and I have to step up and put my boss hat on. "ALRIGHT! One fucking person at a time. I know y'all are pissed, but you know what? Being pissed isn't going to help us find out where this fucker is and figure out what we are going to do. So, be good little boys and ask one at a time." The glares I get in response to my smart-ass comment causes me to clench my ass. I know I'm going to pay for saying it later, but shit they were getting annoying.

After a pregnant pause and about three eye rolls later, Godfrey breaks the silence. "What is his name, Blue? I'm not in the mood for games right now. If he thinks he can encroach on your domain and then threaten you without getting any repercussions, then he is as dumb as he sounds." My eyes widen at how serious Godfrey sounds and shivers overtake me at the chill in his voice. Not wanting to piss him off anymore, I give him all the details he wants and watch as he springs from his seat and stalks to his room.

Everyone else has their lips tightly sealed, but approval is written on their faces. This time it's my turn to roll my eyes. Standing from my spot on the couch, I creep along Godfrey's trail. At the threshold of his door, I look inside and see him pulling drawers open. All types of things come out and go straight into his duffle bag that is laying on his bed — magazines, ammo, sites, and a cleaning kit. Well, I shouldn't have been surprised, my assassin isn't going to let this slide. Not by a long shot.

All his moments are stiff and precise, not wanting to poke the bear further, I creep back to the living room with a look of worry. The mumbling from the rest of the guys quiets as I come into view which only furrows my brow even more. Jaime rises from his spot, walks over to me, and pulls me into his arms. "*Mi amor*, I need you to be more careful. There is only one of you, so please take someone with you next time." Pushing me back some, he runs his hands up to frame my face and locks his gaze with mine.

God, I've missed him. Ever since I was proclaimed the boss, I haven't had time to see him. With Jaime still working for the FBI, they constantly call him, and there are times where he is gone for two to three days at a time. For him to be here now, is honestly a surprise. Not thinking about it anymore, I lean forward and capture his full lips. He meets me halfway and begins to coax my mouth open slowly.

As our kiss deepens, his dick starts to harden against my pelvis and desire pools deep inside me as he starts to nibble on my lip and down my jaw. With my period gone after only three days, I don't hold back on pushing this to where I want it. Trailing my fingers along the seam of his jeans, I find his now fully hardened cock and wrap my hand around the outline. Through the fabric, I start stroking him, steadily pulling groans from him, and fueling the fire that's between us.

I'm so enraptured on what's going on between Jaime and me, that I forget that the rest of my guys are all in the same apartment. That is, until a slap on my ass jars from the sensual embrace. With swollen lips and drenched panties, I twirl to see Godfrey standing behind me with his arms crossed over his chest and a smug fucking look.

Sixteen

NARROWING MY eyes, I start to close the distance between Godfrey and me, but Jaime wraps his arms around my waist and stills me. Dipping down, he dips my ear and then flicks his tongue over the sensitive spot behind my ear, which makes my eyes flutter. Sucking in a breath, I look back at Godfrey whose eyes are blazing with desire and curl my finger at him, motioning for him to come to me.

    Motion to my left draws my attention, with a quick glance, I notice Joe casually advancing with his eyes raking over me like I'm a prize to be won. Flicking my eyes back to Godfrey, I notice that he is in the same exact spot, but this time his knuckles are white as if he is squeezing his fists too tight. I tense at the sight but quickly loosen back up due to Jaime's dick rubbing against my ass. On top of that, Joe starts to run his finger up my side and starts to lazily circle my nipple, which is straining underneath the restrictive material.

Jaime's soft lips connect with my skin again and start trailing from one shoulder to the other. Rolling my head to the side, I give him space to nibble just above where my pulsing artery is. An artery that is beating erratically due to all the desire and need flowing through me. A moan spills from between my lips and at the sound of it, Godfrey moves. Through heavy lids, I watch him approach, like the killer he is. The demons he constantly battles shine bright in his eyes, along with lust—something I wish we could explore more.

Reaching out, he grips my jaw and raises my chin, so I'm looking directly at him. His grip tightens, so tight that there will probably be some kind of bruise; however, I won't fight it, his anger and lust is something I crave. Completely at his mercy, I wait for him to make his next move. Jaime and Joe continue their ministrations and sweet torture, working around the connection between Godfrey and I. With his thumb, Godfrey begins to caress my lips and ease them apart. Wanting to get a taste of him, I subtly flick my tongue out and brush against his fingertip.

With an arched brow from my bold move, he continues to caress my lips, and with each swipe, he coaxes them apart. Puffs of air escape me as I fight back the urge to moan. Joe's tantalizing ministrations on and around my nipples are driving me insane, and Jaime's wandering hands only amplify the need that's inside of me. Godfrey, however, continues to tease me, until he surprises me by sliding his thumb inside my waiting mouth.

Wrapping my lips around his finger, I begin to suck on it as if I was sucking on his dick. He must not have expected my move because he starts to remove it from my greedy little mouth. Not wanting to stop, I sink my teeth into the fleshy tip of his finger and moan as the coppery tang of blood mixes with the lingering taste of salt. Godfrey's heavy eyes widen from the erotic noise coming from me, and he snatches his hand and tucks it safely in his pocket. Joe takes the opportunity to claim my still-parted mouth. His tongue battle should be the only thing I'm thinking of, but all I can think about is everything I plan on doing to Godfrey. That is until Jaime's hand dives inside of my jeans.

His deft fingers work their way under my lace thong and plunge into my drenched pussy. Joe captures the moan that spills out of me as Jaime begins pumping inside of me, and with each stroke, he slides over the hidden sweet spot that's deep inside of me. The weight of my shirt starts to become too much, so with some help from Joe, I rip it over my head leaving my swollen breasts that are cupped by a lace bra in full view for everyone to see. The shirt doesn't even have a chance to touch the ground before Joe is pulling the material of my bra down and latching onto my pert nipple.

Over the noises coming from us, I hear a zipper and someone groaning. Looking over my shoulder, I see Viktor and Frank lounging on the couch with their eyes locked on the scene in front of them. Viktor, however, has his hand stroking his shaft at a languid pace. A gush of desire pools in my core, which intensifies the slick sound from Jaime pumping inside of me. Turning my gaze back to Godfrey, I notice him flicking his eyes from me to the door, as if he can't make up his mind on what to do. Watch me get fucked or hunt down that fucker who threatened to kill me.

Pushing both Jaime and Joe away, I wobble over to Godfrey and pull him down to my height. Though my mind is cloudy with desire and the need to be fucked, I focus on my love for him and his protective ways and whisper to him, "Babe, you hunt that fucker down. If you can't find him, burn his fucking house down. I'll be screaming your name as I come, and whenever you're ready, I'll let you do whatever you want with me." As I speak, I search his eyes for some answers to all the questions I have for him, but instead of finding what I'm looking for, I see a man who will do anything to protect me.

Nodding his head in agreement, he starts to turn toward the door, but with my grasp still on his shirt, I pull him back to me and capture his mouth. I pour my love, desire, and understanding into it, hoping to erase whatever hesitancy he may have. As I pull away, Godfrey reaches around and smacks my ass once again. With the fierce expression I know him for, he says his goodbyes. "I love you, Blue. You don't have to worry when I'm around I'll make him pay." Releasing his shirt, I watch as he charges out of the apartment as if he is ready for battle.

Warm hands slide under my arms and start to palm my breast. Turning in Joe's embrace, I place a finger on his chest and slowly push him back. I don't stop the advancement until we are in the living room and he falls onto the couch. With Frank, Joe, and Viktor in front of me, I look over to Jaime and call him over. "Are you going to finish what you started, *papi*, or are you going to tap out?" I've never fucked all four of them at the same time and recalling the way Jaime acted when Frank was watching, I'm not sure he will participate. When he doesn't make a move, I shrug my shoulders and step in between Joe's legs.

Reaching around my back, I unsnap my bra and let the thin material fall to the floor. My hands trail over my ribs, underneath my breast, and over my nipples. Pinching them between my fingers, I begin to twist and pull at them, causing sweet pain to explode inside of me. With my head thrown back, I feel my long waves of turquoise tickling the small of my back mixing in softness to the sharpness. Releasing my pert buds, I trail my hands down my taut stomach and to the bottom of my jeans. I gaze at each of my men and watch their expressions as I begin to undo the denim material. Latching my thumbs into both my pants and my thong, I begin to push them down leisurely.

Now standing completely naked, I straddle Joe's lap. His hands slide up my sides and cup my breasts. Leaning forward, he takes them into his mouth and begins to lavish them all over again. Tired of watching, Viktor rises to his knees and crawls closer. With each movement he makes, the more I grind against the soft material of Joe's sweatpants which is the only thing keeping me from wrapping my hand around his fucking cock and burying it inside of me. Adding to the movement, Frank starts to scoot closer and then lifts his hips to remove his jeans. The moment they pass his dick, it springs up and bobs in the air, waving like a sign that says *suck me*.

My mouth fills with saliva as I imagine him cramming his dick down my throat and fucking my mouth senseless. Reaching down, I wrap my hands as far as they will go around his dick and start to stroke him, but the desire to have him in my mouth overcomes me. Pulling Joe from my breast with a pop, I lean down and take in as much of Frank as I can. Reaching out, Frank wraps his hands into my locks and holds me down, which blocks off all sources for air. His dick twitches inside of my mouth and bumps my gag reflex, which makes my eyes water, but I don't give in.

With Joe unable to remove his sweats, he nudges Vik who is kneading my ass. "Vik, bro, pull these pants off so I can fuck our girl and grab the lube will ya." Viktor shoots Joe a smirk and stands from the couch. Frank loosens his grip on my head and pulls me back some to allow me to inhale much-needed oxygen, and after a few deep breaths, I start bobbing up and down, making sure to suck his dick like I was sucking his soul out. Lifting my gaze, I see Jaime slowly creeping closer, fighting back a wicked grin, I focus back on pleasing Frank.

A hiss comes from Joe, so I lift up from Frank to find Viktor stroking Joe. His eyes catch mine to gauge my reaction, but my pussy answers for me by gushing with need. Fuck, I didn't know they liked dick! I could've had so much fun with them. With my lip tucked between my teeth, I watch as Viktor leans forward and slides his tongue from the base of Joe's throbbing cock to the purple-tinged tip. Reaching out, Joe turns my attention from what Viktor is doing to look at him. "Princess, we will stop if you want, tell us what you want." Desperation for acceptance sounds in his voice, and his eyes shine as if he is about to lose it all.

Sitting up in his lap, with enough room for Viktor to continue the oral pleasure he is giving to Joe, I ask the only thing I care about. "Do you love him?"

My playful Joe, the man who makes sure I laugh every day, has tears building in his eyes, so with my thumb, I wipe them away. With a deep breath, Joe finally answers, "Yes. I've loved him for over six years. I love both of you, with all of my heart."

"Then that's all I need to know. I love you and Viktor no matter if you like dick or not. Just treat me right and promise I'll get to watch y'all fuck sometimes." Joe's shocked expression turns into laughter at my comment. Seeing that he is back to his joyful self, I resume where I left off. "Viktor, before you go, why don't you line Joe up for me? My pussy is ready to be pounded." I watch as Joe's eyes flutter and then his dick starts to nudge at my parted pussy lips.

Viktor drags Joe's dick up and down my slit making sure it's covered in juices before he puts it at my entrance. Sinking down, I slowly take his dick inside of me, and just before I bottom out, I feel Viktor's knuckles rub against my pussy. With his hand out of the way, Joe slams into me the rest of the way which rips a scream from me. "Ahh fuck, Joe, fuck me, baby!" Gripping my hips, he does just as I ask.

Frank stands from the couch and slides in behind me and pushes me down, so my ass is in the air. Grabbing the lube that Vik just returned with, he pours it down my crack, making sure my puckering rosebud is nice and slick. Joe slows down his thrust and gives Frank enough time to pop the head of his dick past the tight ring and advance the rest of the way. Once I feel his hips against the back of my thighs, I take in a breath to further relax. As if taking that as a cue, they both start moving. In. Out. In. Out. My body writhes with the feeling of their swollen dicks filling me up, and before I know it, I explode. Biting down on Joe's shoulder, I shout out my release, making sure to call the name of the man who would thrive in my pain. "Fuck! Godfrey!" Calling his name doesn't deter my guys, if anything it spurs them on to fuck me harder.

Crawling back on the couch, this time without pants, Viktor scoots with his dick in hand and rubs it against Joe's parted lips. Reaching up, Joe wraps his hand around Vik's dick and guides it into his mouth, and once it's all the way in, Vik starts to pump his hips. My pussy clenches at the sight in front of me which causes Joe to groan which vibrates up Vik's dick where he lets out a groan as well. Fuck, that chain reaction was hot. Looking up to Viktor, I see him looking down at me with a knowing smile.

Movement to the other side of the couch has me whipping my head around. Kneeling with his dick in hand is Jaime. Licking my lips to moisten them, I nudge Jaime's hand out of the way and guide his dick into my waiting mouth. "Ah, fuck, Selene!" Jaime's roar of pleasure tells me everything I need to know. I'm eager to please my men, so just like Frank, I force all of Jaime's dick down my throat, this time, however, I'm not held down. Behind me, Frank's thrusts start to become uneven and harder, and after a few more pumps, he stills as his seed is spilled into my dark channel.

Easing out, Frank places a kiss on the cheek Godfrey reddened and then plops on the opposite couch to watch. Hot cum starts to leak out of the stretched ring, and as I tighten myself, more oozes out. Jaime withdraws his dick from my swollen lips and moves to Frank's previous position. Using the cum as lube, he slides into my already stretched hole and begins to fuck me. Turning back toward Viktor and Joe, I lean over and flick my tongue out to where they are connected. I alternate between kissing the side of Joe's mouth to sucking on the side of Viktor's dick, but as Viktor starts to come, he pulls out and places his dick between both Joe's and my mouth.

Hot cum ejects from Viktor's cock and lands inside and around my mouth. Swallowing whatever made it inside, I start to lick the rest away, but Joe brings me closer and licks the cum away for me. Flicking my tongue out, I do the same for him and swallow it all away. Pulling away from them, I look over my shoulder to Jaime who is plunging in and out of me out of rhythm with Joe, so I'm having a hard time reaching the orgasm that is hanging right in front of me. Squeezing my muscles, I pull a hiss from both Jaime and Joe. Next thing I know, Joe is fucking me harder and then they get into sync.

My orgasm comes crashing into me and makes everything around me explode. White spots flash in front of my vision, and with both of them still fucking me, it only drags out the euphoric feeling. Joe starts to falter and with three more thrusts, he comes, filling my greedy pussy with his seed. Reaching under me, Jaime runs his fingers over my clit, which makes me twitch from having two orgasms back to back. But he doesn't stop, no, he strums my clit while he continues to fuck my stretched hole.

Another orgasm starts to build inside of me, but I know I can't reach it, I'm so fatigued, and two is enough, so I start to shake my head. "Fuck, *papi*, I can't, I can't have another one."

"Yes you can, I can feel you tightening your little ass around my dick. Give me one more, Selene, and then I'll let you rest." Jaime's pleas for another one seems out of this fucking world, but as he continues to stimulate my clit, I feel the bomb inside of me growing. Joe pushes me up so he can get to my breast and then takes one into his mouth, nibbling and sucking on my pebbled nub. With his dick still semihard and nestled in my pussy, I clench around it which causes him to bite my nipple, and at the same time, Jaime pinches my clit. The dual stimulation does it for me, and once again, I explode.

Jaime spills his seed inside of me, allowing it to mix with Frank's, and after his cum is done jetting out, he gently slides out of me. Collapsing down onto Joe, I take a deep breath and try to slow my heart. My body feels so deliciously used, and every channel is filled with the essence of my men. Nestling deeper into Joe's embrace, I call out to all my men. "I love you guys. Forever and always." As their "I love yous" sound back, I let the fatigue take over and pass out.

Seventeen

Bang.
    Bang.
    Bang.
    "What the fuck do you want?!" Frank's groggy voice calls out to whoever fucking woke us. I try rolling over and blocking out the noise, but the door swings open showing Viktor who is pulling on a shirt. Reaching out, I grab my phone and check the time. Shit, it's way too early for all this.
    "There was a break-in at the compound, and the dogs got the intruder. We need to get down there to handle the shit." Groaning in frustration, I throw off my blanket and pull on my jeans from earlier. Skipping the bra, I pull on one of Frank's tees and toss Frank his jeans so he can get dressed as well. As I push past Viktor to get to the bathroom, I give him a chaste kiss and then straighten myself up, so I don't look like I just got out of bed.

With my hair in a bun, I turn towards Frank who is sliding a shirt on, and inwardly sighs in disappointment as his lickable abs disappear. Geez, I just had three orgasms, and I'm already ready for more—such a fucking horny bitch. Shaking my head at my inner monologue, I head to the fridge and pull out my favorite energy drink. I need fucking wings, and one sixteen-ounce can will do it. Sitting at the table, pop the top and start to gulp my drink down. One by one, Viktor, Jaime, Frank, and Joe emerge from their rooms.

We are about to head out the front door when it creeps open revealing Godfrey, who has soot lines on his face. His eyes rise in surprise to see us all awake and dressed, but Viktor fills him in on our situation. Nodding his head, he walks over to me and wraps me in a tight embrace. The second I bury my face into his chest, I get overwhelmed with the smell of smoke. Pulling back, I look up to him with a questioning gaze and say, "I take it you found his home and burned it down?"

"I did. He had poor security, and everyone who was inside was sleeping. However, the imbecile was nowhere to be found, so I placed cameras to give me a live feed of his estate. I'm sure he will be coming back, and if I can get his tag or car description, I can hunt him down."

"You did a perfect job then, my love. Now, go get showered and rest. We will handle this tonight." Pulling him down, I give him a goodnight kiss and then walk out the door with the rest of my guys in tow. With it being so early in the morning, no one is wandering around or driving, so we make it to the compound pretty quickly. As the gates start to pull apart, we are presented with a group of guards and their dogs surrounding who I presume is the intruder. Parking a few feet away, I hop out and approach the scene.

As the guards part, I notice the snarling rottweilers, Cujo and Roscoe, snap their teeth at a petite woman who is sitting on her knees. Huh, not what I expected. With my arms crossed over my chest, I start my interrogation. "Who the fuck are you, and what the fuck are you doing?"

The woman flicks her eyes over to me and sneers. "Go fuck yourself!" Being the dumb cunt that she is, she hocks a loogie and nearly hits me. As soon as the spit leaves her mouth, one of the guards smacks her in the face with the butt of his automatic rifle, which makes the intruder fall to the ground.

"Did anyone search her? Did she not have an ID or a phone?" The guards all look to each other and come up with nothing. Muttering to myself how useless these fuckers are, I stomp over to where the bitch lays and pat her down. I end up finding a phone, flashlight, pocket knife, and a small handgun. With everything I pull from her pockets, the more I get pissed. What the fuck are we paying these people for? With her gun in hand, I jump to my feet and open fire at the closest person. The guard who was hit drops to the ground and everyone starts to shout. Aiming at the sky, I fire again, which causes everyone to quiet. "Do you see this fucking gun? This was on her! You did not do your job! She could have killed you all or worse, ME! Everyone here is on three-month probation and must be retrained. IS THAT UNDERSTOOD?!"

I'm shaking with anger as they all drop their heads in shame. Turning back to the intruder, I spot her on her hands and knees, trying to get away. Stomping over to the guard who holds Cujo's and Rosco's leashes, I yank them from him and set the dogs free. With two simple words, they are off. "Get her." The two specially-trained dogs bound from their spots and tackle the woman to the ground. Screams fill the night along with the sound of growls coming from my beasts. The guards all look uneasy as they start to shuffle from one foot to another, but my guys and I are all smiling like fucking fiends.

While the dogs continue their carnage, I pick up the bitch's phone and open it up. Fuck, facial recognition is needed. Hmm, let's hope the dogs didn't completely destroy her face. I wait until the screaming stops to call the dogs back, and as they walk away, I see the mangled state she is now in. Blood is pooled all over the dirt, and pieces of flesh litter the ground. With my luck, her face isn't that fucked-up, so I squat down, aim the phone at her and wait for it to unlock. Once I gain access, I stand up and start to dig for information.

Letting my guys handle the rest, I make my way over to the SUV. Not long after, they climb in, and I give them the low down. "The cunt's name was Nikki, and she was from Colorado. Her recent calls are all to the same person so we will have Godfrey track who it is. According to her text messages, she was here to gain intel on what we had and to destroy whatever she could.

My name is mentioned in a couple of the messages, but they seem to be focused on the fact that I'm with Frank and she was pretty much butt hurt about the whole situation." My eyes flick over to Frank to find him with a blank expression. Arching a brow, I wait for his response.

Letting out a sigh of frustration, Frank breaks and spills his secret. "She was one of my frequent fucks a couple of years ago, but she started to get too attached, so I cut her loose. That is all there is to tell." With a shrug, he turns back to the road and drives us back to our apartment. I don't say anything about Frank's confession, and neither do the guys. But as we all settle in for the night once again, I start to make my way to Joe's room when Frank grabs my arm and stops me. "You're sleeping with me. Don't let a dead bitch who is part of my past get between us."

Scrunching my face, I try to deny that I was letting his past bother me, but I can't lie to myself. "You're right, I'm sorry. Jealousy was rearing her ugly face. But don't worry, I knocked the bitch down."

"Good, now come on, we got an early morning, so a few more hours of sleep is needed." With a smack on my ass, he leads me to his room where we strip back down to nothing and climb into bed. With both of us in our spooning positions, Frank wraps his arm around my waist and pulls me closer to him. As I start to wiggle to get closer, his dick starts to harden and begins to press against my back.

Rolling over onto my back, I look over to Frank, who is gazing down at me with a spark in his eyes. Reaching up, I start to trace the hard lines of his cheek and run my fingers through his recently trimmed beard. "I love you, Frank." My declaration may only be a whisper, but those four words are a shout from my soul and a declaration of my commitment.

Leaning over, Frank hovers just above my face, our lips nearly brushing each other and our breath mixing together. The smile on his face is one like I have never seen before — a deep-set dimple and a slight blush pinkening his cheeks. Finally, after what seems like forever, he utters a reply, "My queen, I have loved you since the moment I laid eyes on you, and I plan to love you until the end of time." With Frank's deep baritone voice, his words came out almost like a growl.

His kisses are slow yet precise, full of passion, and gentle. He doesn't try to dominate me or bite my lips; instead, he lavishes me in sweet kisses, leaving trails of his love everywhere he goes. Working from my mouth, he heads to my jaw and then down to my collarbone. As he nips at my collarbone, he trails his hand down my stomach, over my mound and begins to trace the seam of my pussy.

I spread my legs to invite him to continue, but instead of slipping inside of my greedy channel, he proceeds to stroke my skin with a feather-like touch. Moving down to my chest, he traces the outside of my areola but ignores my nipples which are begging for attention and then continues down my stomach. When he reaches my hips, he nips my pale skin from one side to another, leaving small red marks in his wake. By now, I'm panting with desire; my core is quivering with the need to be filled, and wetness pools between my legs.

As he starts to move closer to my core, I hold my breath in anticipation. The thought of having his talented tongue working my clit is all I can think about, and it's nearly driving me crazy. He reaches the top of my slit and stills, but to my dismay, he veers to the side and begins kissing all around where I need him. I nearly scream in frustration, but I know he wants to take this slow and make it more than just a fuck. Frank is never slow like this, usually the one to just take what he wants, so for him to show my body appreciation like this is a rare treasure that I don't want to ruin.

I'm nearly blue with anticipation by the time he hovers over my slit. Darting his tongue out, he separates my folds and hums in satisfaction as he laps at the juices that are waiting for him. Kneeling between my legs, he tosses my legs over his shoulders and begins to devour me. Each flick of his tongue brings moans, whimpers, and cries of pleasure out of me, and after only a few seconds of his sweet pleasure, I orgasm. The blissful *O* relaxes my body and fills me with endorphins, making my channel overflow with sweet nectar.

Leaning up, Frank licks away my juices that cover his mouth and then rises, so his dick is lined up with my entrance. Lifting my head, I watch with fascination as he grasps his dick and begins to push inside of me. The way my channel stretches to accommodate his thick dick is something to marvel over, and once he is completely seated, he throws his head back, letting out a string of curses. "Fuck Selene, your pussy is so fucking tight and so fucking perfect. I swear it's made just for me." Leaning down, he braces himself with his arms on either side of me and begins to pump into me at a leisurely pace.

We both get lost in each other, and with every change in position, the ball deep inside of me expands. Not able to hold off anymore, I push Frank to his back and ride him. My hips undulate in an exquisite motion, bringing me closer the orgasm that has been lingering in front of me. With each movement, I climb, nearing the edge, but I just can't reach it. With my whimper of frustration, Frank places his thumb over my swollen clit and begins to strum. My channel clenches around his shaft like a vice grip, and with a grunt, Frank begins to thrust, slamming out pelvises together. The slow lovemaking is thrown out the window as we both chase our release. My movements start to falter as I feel the impending explosion, and with a pinch to my clit, I surrender to bliss.

Frank moves his hands to my hips and grips them to steady me as he continues to pump into me. Each thrust prolongs my euphoric state, and with a grunt, he spurts inside of me — scorching my channel with his seed. With his release of my hips, I collapse on top of him and pant from exertion. Below me, Frank's abs quiver, and his breath hitches. Pulling out of my sore channel, he slides to the side and rolls to his nightstand.

Flopping on my back, I throw my arm over my face and steady my breathing, but as Frank rolls back over to me, he removes my arm and smiles down at me. His grin is like a kid in a candy store and like he is totally up to something. Pushing myself up, I lean on my elbows and question him. "What's got you all giddy?"

Instead of answering me, Frank rises to his knees and pulls his hands from behind his back. I freeze as I see the black velvet box that is cradled in his hands. Sitting up the rest of the way, I stare at the box, scared of what this could mean. I don't want to overthink this; it can be anything. Frank reaches out, takes my left hand which is clammier than a freaking clam, and places a chaste kiss on my knuckles. With a deep breath, he breaks the silence. "Selene, I love you more than life, and I truly want to spend forever with you. I talked it over with the guys, and they support this completely. So, will you, Selene Romanov, marry me?" A squeal escapes me as I nearly tackle him and knock him back into the bed.

"Are you serious? You want to marry me? Like forever?"

"Forever Selene, I'm not going anywhere."

With tears running down my face, I say what my heart is already screaming. "Yes! Yes! Yes! Yes, I will marry you!" Opening the box, I see a brilliant princess cut diamond on a diamond-encrusted silver band and squeal once again. My hand is shaking so bad, Frank has to still me as he slides the engagement ring on my finger and as soon as it slides into place, I tackle Frank once again, making sure to wrap him in my arms and plan never to let go.

Eighteen

I CAN'T stop staring at the glistening stone on my finger. Never in a million years did I ever think I would ever get engaged, let alone married. So waking up and seeing that it wasn't a dream made me forget the fact I only slept for a total of maybe three hours. As much as I would like to sleep in, I have to meet Doris to ask her who Jelena is and why the girl in the picture looks like me. After a quick shower, I creep out of the house and make my way to the parking garage.

I'm not even two minutes into my trip when my phone starts to vibrate in the center console. The name on the caller ID makes me roll my eyes, and as much as I don't want to answer, I do. "Hello Devoy, what do I owe the pleasure?"

"Ms. Selene, I hope all is well with you."

"Hmm, things are perfectly peachy, now what can I do for you?"

Sighing, he says, "Always cutting the

niceties short. There was a house fire last night, do you happen to know anything about it?"

"Now why would I know anything about it? I'm not into fire play if that's what you're getting at Mr. Devoy." My sarcasm is so thick, I can hear Devoy choking on it.

"Right, well the owner of the house is pretty adamant you're the cause, said you are probably upset with a business deal?"

"Look, Devoy, I know you're just doing your job, but I have shit to do. So if you want to continue getting paid, I advise you to drop this conversation and push the file in a dark and dusty place."

"As much as I would like to do that, I have my higher-ups breathing down my neck at the increase of gang activity and violence. I want it to be known, Selene, that when Dominik was alive, things like this didn't happen. He had things under control. So why don't you take a lesson from his old ways?"

"Or what, Devoy? You can't do anything to me, and you know it. I own you!"

"You don't own me, Selene. I worked with Dominik because it was beneficial for both of us, now it's not. So take this as your final warning."

With the call ended, I dial my lawyer and give him a quick recap of the conversation. He let me go so he can get a head start on putting a lid on the events and drawing up whatever documents he may need to keep Devoy quiet. Not wanting to leave my guys in the dark, I send them a text with the same information.

By the time I pull up to the diner, my nerves are on the fritz, from not only Devoy's call but what Doris has to tell me. I know I'm not their child and I have no relation, but still, I considered Dominik as my father, so knowing he had a secret like this blows. Blowing out a breath, I reach over and grab the envelope that holds the picture and a clipping from the newspaper, along with the cemetery information for Jelena's grave. As I slide out of my truck, I'm blinded by the glaring sun, which is a constant reminder that summer is fast approaching. Using my hand as a visor, I head into the diner to get this over with.

Walking through the door causes the chime to sound, announcing the presence of another customer, but instead of listening to the sign that says *please wait to be seated*, I glide through the tables and come to a stop where Doris is sitting. Dressed in a red plaid top and jeans, sits the woman who Dominik loved. With her face buried in her hands, I doubt she noticed my approach, so I just slide in the booth and say, "Whatever it is, it can't be that bad."

Jumping in her seat, she looks at me wide-eyed and stutters her reply. "S-Selene, I didn't see you come in. I'm sorry, you're right, love. It's just been a long time since I've had to dig up these memories. So forgive me if I don't seem like myself."

Leaning back in the booth, I wave off her worry and voice my concerns. "No reason to apologize Doris. I really don't mean to put you through this, but I have to get answers. I have so many questions, and with Dominik no longer here to answer them, I have to go to my next option—Doyle and you."

Letting out a snort, she shakes her head and reaches for her coffee. "That man needs to find a new profession. I'm surprised he is still staying afloat. After all, Dominik was his only client."

I can't help but nod in understanding. The one and only time I went to his office, I thought I was at an abandoned building. "Well, I guess he will be around for a little bit longer. I took over Dom's account with him since Doyle knows all the ins and outs." My mind races on a million ways I can start this conversation. I don't want to cause Doris any distress because she has been nothing but nice to me, but there are too many unanswered questions. "Doris . . ."

"Good morning, ma'am! Sorry for taking so long, I didn't realize anyone came inside. What can I get you on this fine morning?" Standing with the brightest smile and her notepad ready to go is a perky, middle-aged brunette. Everything about her is so happy and chipper, from her bright yellow nail polish to her perfectly pinned-up hair. With a quick glance, I scope out her name. Gloria.

Well shit, her spunky personality has me feeling all chipper already. Shooting our server a grin, I order my breakfast and get Doris's as well. Boiled eggs and chicken for me and bacon, lettuce, tomato, and egg sandwich for Doris. After the server bounces away, I look back to Doris and continue where I left off. "Doris, did you and Dominik have a child together? Is that why he was so quick with taking me in? Because she would have looked like me?"

Dropping her head with a sigh, she begins to twiddle her fingers and then looks up to me and utters in a broken voice, "Yes, we did. Her name was Jelena, and she was our world. Dominik loved her more than life and was even going to give up the lifestyle he lived for her." The silence between us is definitely needed. For me to absorb what she just said and for Doris to collect her thoughts, but the silence didn't last long. "She was only ten when it happened. The car just came out of nowhere and collided with us. The cops said it was a drunk driver, but we knew different. He was aiming for us head-on. Since that night, Dominik dove headfirst into the world you know and quickly rose to the top. Fueled by anger and hatred for everyone. That is until he met you."

Tears threaten to spill out her aged eyes, the worry line more prominent now than before, and her thinned lips quiver from all the emotion she is holding in. I have no words for what she just told me, I mean, I'm shocked for sure. I would never have imagined Dominik leaving the business, let alone him having a child. "So what happened between you and him? I mean, y'all had a child together. Yet, he never mentioned you or Jelena in all the years I knew him." I know losing a child could be hard for parents, but why separate? I just don't get it.

Her lips thin at my question but with a prolonged sigh, she answers, "I left because I couldn't handle all the violence. Dominik went on a killing spree until he could find the man responsible for our tragedy. Though I'm grateful that the bastard suffered, I don't have a mean bone in my body, so supporting his ways was not something I could do. As for why he never mentioned us, well that's simple. I made him swear not to. I wanted a peaceful life away from it all, and I didn't want our daughter's name to be dragged through the filth that he worked with."

"That's completely reasonable. I know he loved you, though. He might not have said it to me, but the way he looked when I mentioned him to you, well it was one of a man in love." Doris smiles at me with a grin full of love and happiness. Nothing about it is fake and knowing that Dominik loved her, makes me believe she still loves him. Almost like true love.

The server chooses that moment to bring out food and thank god she did. I don't know how much longer I can go without chowing down. We wait until the server drops our food off and enters into the staff-only door before we say another word. "We knew each other since college. He just came over from Russia and was in one of my classes. It was like instalove. We couldn't get enough of each other, but as time went on, he started to change. I will always love him, regardless if we were together or not, and he knew that." With every word, her voice cracked, and I knew the battle to hold the tears in was a losing one. Reaching over, I grab some napkins and hand them to her.

Once her tears are dry, she continues. "You know Jelena was the reason he took you in under his wings. She looked just like you—from your thick, wavy hair to your freckle-covered cheeks, and hell, even your resilient attitude. Part of me thinks it's because he pretended you were her."

"God, I hope not! As much as that would

mean to me, I don't think he would want his *daughter* working as an escort." I've lived a fucked-up life, and I don't regret anything about it, but I know damn well if I ever have kids, I would do anything possible for them not to be like me.

"Tsk, tsk, tsk. Dominik thought highly of you and respected you. He knew he wasn't your father and he couldn't tell you what to do in that aspect, but you also have to remember, he was the boss of thousands of people. He couldn't show any sympathy or favoritism toward you. There were too many things that could happen if he did." Clasping her hands, she looks out the window and toward the brilliant blue sky. "You know, he came here nearly every week to talk about you with me. Those moments helped me live without our baby, a balm if you will."

Staring down at my plate, I push around the bits of food that's left and fumble with what to say next. "I mean . . . you're welcome? I don't know what to say to all this. Of course, I had some inclination that there is something going on, from the photo to the gravestone. I guess I needed to hear it myself. Like I said before, he was like a father to me."

"You . . . You have a picture? Can I see?" The pleading look in Doris's eyes makes me feel bad for not mentioning it earlier. Pulling the envelope out of my purse, I hand it over and watch as she grabs it with shaky hands. Her nimble fingers slide it open and gently pull both the clipping and photo out. With the envelope forgotten, she covers her mouth and gasps, "Oh my gosh! I thought these were lost so long ago!

Please, oh please, Selene, can I have them?" Tears streak down her cheeks in a steady stream, marring her makeup and dripping to her white blouse.

"Who am I to say no to you? They belong to you anyways, so please, take them. They were in a secret compartment in Dominik's desk, and as I was cleaning it out, I discovered them. Oh, the cemetery where both Jelena and Dominik are buried are well taken care of. The caretaker will look over them for as long as he can." Doris doesn't look at me while I'm talking to her; instead, she stares at the picture with a look of pure joy on her face.

Pushing my plate to the side, I fold my arms on the table and bathe in the feeling of accomplishment. The chime sounds as someone enters the diner, so out of automatic response, I flick my eyes over to check out whoever it was. With one glance, I go on high alert. The guy is hunched over, dressed in all black with something bulky underneath his coat. Ever since the mall incident, I became more aware of what's going on around me, and getting shot is not something I was to deal with. This blip on my radar darts his eyes all over the place, making sure not to stare at one place for too long. After a few seconds, he makes his way to the bathrooms and disappears.

My gut is yelling at me that something is fishy about the whole situation, so I pull my phone out and send an urgent text to my guys. My body becomes itchy with the need to leave, my foot starts to tap uncontrollably, and my fingers tap in quick succession on the hard tabletop. A hand waving in my peripheral catch my attention, so I jerk to see who it is. "Selene, are you okay? You look like you just saw a ghost." Concern laces Doris's voice as if she can sense my inner turmoil.

With the guy still hidden in the bathroom and the diner empty except for Doris and me, I decide to make my move. "Doris, we need to leave. Don't ask questions, don't look back, just get your ass out of here." Her eyes widen with shock, but without missing a beat, she quickly gathers her stuff and power walks out. Standing from the booth, I toss a hundred on the table and start to exit the diner, but before I can reach the exit, the man emerges, holding a blazing glass bottle. A fucking Molotov.

It seems as if the world slows down to a minuscule crawl when I spot the bottle. Everything that can happen flashes before my eyes and my brain starts to misfire on what to do next. *RUN! RUN! RUN!* No matter how much I scream at myself to move, I can't. The man has pure evil all over his face, and the grin he has intensifies everything which makes fear run through me. *Shit, I'm going to die.* My brain switches focus from the flame to the movement in his arm, which is rearing back for him to toss the bomb. Even as his Molotov welding arm starts to fly forward, I can't get myself to move. But as I watch his fingers slide off of the glass bottle and the bomb becomes airborne, everything speeds up to a normal pace. With no time to spare, I fling myself behind the reception desk and duck behind the wooden podium.

The bottle explodes and a scorching inferno

envelopes me. The heat from the fire burns my skin, and my body's natural defense kicks in, causing sweat to pour off of me. Thankfully, whatever accelerant this fucker used burned up quickly and with the help of the fire alarm and the diner's sprinkler system, it was put out just as fast. Pulling my gun from my holster, I peek around the charred podium to spot the bomber loading yet another bomb. There's no way in hell I can withstand another blast!

With three steadying breaths, I roll out from my cover and get to my knee. After all the time I spent with Frank practicing my aim, now is the time it comes into play. Like muscle memory, I aim and pull the trigger. My shot waivers a little to the left and hits the man in the arm, making him drop the lighter that was in hand and without waiting for him to surrender, I continue to shoot. My main objection was to secure my safety, but now, I will fucking kill him.

Nineteen

THE AC from the back of the ambulance cools my skin from the irritating scorch obtained from the bombing, and the burn cream the paramedics gave me is now slathered on the blisters with the hopes to reduce them. They wanted to take me to the hospital, but I flat out refused to go, though. But with Director Devoy approaching me with such a pissy look, I might just change my mind. As he gets closer, he waves the medics away and ensures there aren't any prying ears.

His wrinkled eyes give me a once-over, and once he sees that I'm okay, he shakes his head and pulls out his notebook. With a click of his pen, he begins his interrogation. "Miss Selene, or should I say, Missus?" His eyes signal down to the glistening diamond band on my finger with speculation, so to sidestep any further questions, I cross my stiff arms and hide the ring.

"It's Miss, for now. So are you here to take my statement and send me on my merry way?"

With pursed lips, he flips open his notepad and takes down all of my recounted details. By the time he gets done, he is left with more questions than I care to answer. "Remember, Devoy; your fancy car over there wouldn't be possible without me, so make sure that statement is all pretty and airtight."

With stiff movements, Devoy closes his notepad and crosses his arms, almost like he is a defiant toddler. Arching a brow, I wait for him to throw a hissy fit and right on cue, he does. "And you need to remember the chat we had not even two hours ago! Selene, there have been too many incidents so close together. There's only so much fudging I can do before someone else gets wind of it and comes down here to investigate. You need to get your shit together!"

With all the pain forgotten, I jump off the back of the ambulance and get all up in his bubble. "Who the fuck do you think you're talking to, Devoy! I may not be Dominik or a man, but they are, and they will fuck you up without question." Every word is a snarl and a close attempt to knock Devoy flat on his ass; however, when I mention them, he jerks his attention behind me and stumbles. Frank, Joe, Viktor, Godfrey, and Jaime are all standing side by side with matching menacing grins. Add their muscles straining against their shirts, and they look even more intense.

Balling his hands into fists, he turns back to me and says, "I will not let this continue. I want out. No more. I can't run my unit properly with this guilt on my conscious. From here on out, we are done. No worries though, I will keep

Dominik's promise. Everything that happened prior to now is nonexistent. But that's it! You have done nothing but cause chaos left and right. Murders, arson, drug cartels, and so much fucking more." I watch as the vein in his forehead bulges and his face contorts into a malicious gleam. "I'll be watching you, Selene. Remember that." With his threat, he turns back around and marches toward my men and pushes his way through them.

My blood is boiling with anger and the need to make him fucking pay. He would be six feet deep by now if all these fucking people weren't here. Shaking my head in frustration, I walk over to Godfrey. "You will watch him. I want his lines tapped and someone monitoring his web usage. I will not be played. Oh and Godfrey, you are NOT to kill him. I need him alive and with the shit that's going down, he will come crawling back."

Godfrey stares down at me with rage burning in his eyes, I know he is nearly bursting at the seems to get some blood on his hands, but I can't let him. I arch a brow waiting for him to object, but instead, he grips my neck, pulls me closer to him, and slams his mouth to mine. Everything about our kiss is savage, from the biting of the lips to the thrashing on his tongue. With a slight adjustment of his hand, he places his forefinger and his thumb over both of my carotids, blocking the blood flow. My mind starts to get foggy, and as my knees start to buckle, he releases my neck. With his arm wrapped around my waist, he holds me up while my head starts to clear.

With my bearings back to normal, I straighten myself up and push away from Godfrey. I start to smile at him, but a sharp pain makes me wince. Darting my tongue out, I realize I have a busted lip that was fine before Godfrey got ahold of me. "Now was that called for?"

"It will remind you to stay out of trouble and to behave yourself. We don't like finding out that you not only snuck out of the house, but also went somewhere unsupervised, and were attacked on top of it. Let's not forget you promised to take someone with you. You lied." Well shit, now I feel bad for not waking someone. Dropping my gaze, I stare at the ground and lace my fingers together. Godfrey's hand runs down my arm and grasps my left hand. I freeze as he brings the engagement ring into view. I know Frank said they all approve, but hurting others is not something I want.

Hesitantly, I raise my gaze to look up at Godfrey, and what I find makes me instantly relax. The murderous gaze is pushed aside for one of love, and his smile is quirked to the side, which makes his dimple pop. I watch as he raises my hand to his lips and lingers just above it. His words are barely a whisper, but before he places a gentle kiss on the diamond band, he says, "Soon, my love." My heart stutters and my soul swoons with his words, but before I can say anything to him, our moment is interrupted.

"Oh, Selene! You crazy girl, what were you thinking?! You could have died!" Doris's frantic shouting has me turning toward her to apologize, but when I see her, I choke on my words. The loving woman looks like she is about to tear me a new one, and once I spot the shoe she is waving in her hand, I clench my butt in anticipation of being spanked. I look toward my guys for help, but they just glare, showing me that they are on her side. Looking over my shoulder for Godfrey, I notice him backing away to leave the scene. The paramedics shake their heads and hop back into the ambulance, and the cops only give me a glance and return to their interview and investigation. Shit.

"Doris, I'm . . ." The words are halted, and my jaw slams closed as she wraps her loving arms around me and squeezes me to her motherly bosom. I nearly fall because of our height difference, but her strong grip on me tightens, so I don't. With no sign of her letting go, I wrap my arms around her. Her plump body shakes, and with all the strength I can muster, I look up to her face. Tears stream down her cheeks and my heart breaks for her.

Breaking out of her hold, I pull her to my chest and try to calm her down. "Shh, Doris; it's fine. I had to get you out. I swear, I'm fine. Just a little scald from the explosion."

"It's not okay! You're just like him, always putting yourself in danger for everyone else. You're not a superhero, Selene, and I'm not looking forward to going to another funeral anytime soon!" Her tears soak my shirt, and her words knock me down to the deepest recesses of my mind. She's right. Fuck, everyone is right. I was lucky that I got away with just minor burns. These past few months have had too many close calls for me. I'm not ready to leave this world yet either. I have five men I want to spend the rest of my life with.

With my chin resting on her unruly silver waves, I look over to my men who are all huddled in a circle and then slide my gaze over to the frantic waitress and line cook, who are being questioned by the police. As if pushing away the sadness from losing Dominik wasn't hard enough, now I need to find me a cup of *man the fuck up* and become the savage that's needed to eliminate the threats. "Doris, I'm not going to promise you that I won't have close calls like this again, but I will promise you that I will never purposely put myself in the line of fire again. But you need to know, I am like Dominik. I won't back down and let these fuckers run me down."

The woman in my arms stills. Raising her red, puffy eyes, she looks at me with lifelong sorrow. Her lips thin and her worn hands rise to brace by face. "I may not like what you're saying, but I will be there for you until the very end." I fear that she will resent me for the things I have to do and knowing she couldn't be around Dom because of this lifestyle, adds a certain level of fear. This woman has been kind to me, and with our few interactions, she has shown me the kind of love a mother would show her own.

Giving her one last hug, I separate from her and head over to where Frank, Viktor, and Joe are standing. My gaze darts for my missing love, but I don't see him. Seeing my concern, Joe answers my silent question. "Jaime got a call and had to leave."

"Was it the agency?"

"He didn't say; he couldn't even give a time

on when he would be back." Pulling me to his side, Joe kisses the top of my head, and then I'm tugged to the next. Each one of them pulls me into their arms and makes some kind of connection with me. I guess the events from today shook them more than I thought.

I don't fight their need to have me close, and after Frank lets me go, I look them all over and start to plan how I'm going to get my retribution. What I do know is that at this moment, the crime scene is full of people, and the reporters are starting to show. But anything I have to say to them has to wait until we get somewhere safe. "Frank, check with the head investigator and tell him we are leaving. We need to talk. All of us." With the nod of understanding from the three of them, I head over to where their SUV is with Joe and Vik trailing behind me.

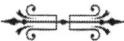

AN HOUR later, we are all huddled in my office except for Jaime and Godfrey, both of which will be caught up when they are done with whatever they are doing. My office chair swivels and creaks slightly under my weight as I recline back and mindlessly rotate myself side to side. Frank, Viktor, and Joe are scattered around the office, either sitting, leaning against the wall, or browsing the array of books on the shelves behind me. We have been in this soundproof room for nearly five minutes, and no one has made a sound.

Sighing, I lean forward and rest my arms on the desk and decide to lay my plan out. "So there's going to be some changes. We can't let people like the one who attacked me in our territory. I know it's next to impossible to know who is working for who, but preventative measures must be made. We all know this is only going to get worse the closer we get to the end of the two weeks that fucking bastard gave me. So first things first, I want Octavia sent somewhere safe. She has too much post-traumatic stress as it is, and any more attacks will only make it worse. I want someone to find an 'in' for the traffic center, more specifically where the street cameras are being monitored. I want surveillance put out for Giovanni Moretti. I want to know where he eats, where he shits, and who his inside people are. His suppliers need to be found, and they either need to be brought over to use or destroyed. That's the only option they have."

"Find his weak spots, whatever will break him. I don't care what it is. We need to bring him down, and we need to do it fast. I will not risk Dominik's livelihood being destroyed within the first fucking year! While I'm thinking of it, I want Sasha brought in. Give him a fucking raise if we have to. But I want him on our side when this shit blows up, and it *will* blow up. Let's not pretend it won't." Every word that comes from me is with the authority I demand, but with the respect my men deserve. We are a team, so having them at my side during these trying times is crucial.

I look out to my men and watch them take in what I said, and with each passing second, my gut twists more, making me even more nauseous than I was from the adrenaline caused by the bombing. Frank's hand slides onto my shoulder and gives me a squeeze. Turning my attention to him, I wait for him to say something and when he does, it strikes true and understanding. "Selene, you are not only the woman who we wish to spend the rest of our lives with but the woman who runs the organization that brought us all together. When we all joined, we knew this wasn't going to be about saving puppies and helping old women cross the street. So everything you are asking of us, is something we are willing to do without a question and if there is ever a time what you're saying doesn't make sense, we will let you know. So trust us when we say we got you and shit will get done."

Pushing off the wall he was leaning on, Joe approaches the desk and says, "I called Godfrey and relayed the message to him so he can get started on the tech side. As for me, I'm sure I have a worker who can get the inside scoop at the traffic center."

"While he does that, I'll call Sasha. I'm sure he won't be hard to get full-time, not with you being the one who is asking." I can't help but roll my eyes at Viktor's undeniably truthful statement, and as much as I want to deny it, knowing that I'm going to see Sasha again sends tingles through me. He is like the forbidden fruit, one that is pretty to look at but that's about it.

With everyone on board and giving me all the support I could ever ask for, I rise from my desk, grasp Frank's hand with my engagement ring on full display and say, "I love each and every one of you, so knowing that you guys are going to stick by me in this chaos, is something that I can never thank you enough. But now that we all have our own personal missions, let's get this shit going. We have a fucking slimy meatball to hunt down and demolish."

Twenty

THE PAST week has been nothing but chaos and headaches. Ever since the bombing, there has been some kind of attack nearly every day, ranging from drive-by shootings, loiterings, multiple overdoses, and increased murders. Not only has the crime increased, but the police activity has also. I've spotted Devoy patrolling in his black Mercedes and lingering outside the club a few times but never once has he gotten out of his vehicle to approach me. With his recent appearances, I bet on one of the two things are going to happen: either he is going to make his move soon and try to make an arrest, or he is going to come crawling back, begging for mercy to return the funds that he is used to living off. The question is, when will either option take place.

"Ma'am, your drink." The courteous voice brings me back from wandering thoughts, and as I turn toward the owner of it, I blink away my dazed expression. Standing in only white leather chaps is one of the newer servers that I recently hired to work at Sub Rosa. He's a pretty boy which makes him easy on the eyes, but what makes him one of the top tipped already, is the fact all the cougars go crazy over him. Hell, I'm not even thirty, and he has me flustered with the way he rolls his tongue when he talks.

Looking over to the tray in his hand, I notice two shot glasses with clear liquid, a salt shaker, and a bowl of lemon wedges. "Just put them on the stand and remove the other ones. Go ahead and get me another round." I've already downed four shots, what's four more. Hell, it's not like I have anything else to do tonight besides be here since I'm hosting this fucking event. An event that was planned by Dominik before he passed so canceling it didn't sit right with me. Tonight's theme is Cowboys and Corsets. Hence why server boy is baring his ass in those fucking chaps and why I'm this old western white lace saloon dress.

The server does what I ask, and I quickly down the shots. The burn disappeared after the second shot, and so did my care for looking ladylike left by the third. With the last one downed, I use the back of my hand to wipe away the excess and then look over toward my men. To my surprise, I spot Viktor and Joe engaged in a passionate kiss in the dark corner. I get lost in watching the way they grind against each other and the way Joe throws his head back as Viktor begins to stroke Joe's dick through his jeans. The sight that I'm devouring makes desire swell inside of me and with the alcohol flowing through my system, everything starts to tingle.

With the tingles zinging straight to my core, I begin to shift in my throne with the hopes to alleviate some of the sensations, but the friction only does the opposite and makes it worse. Out of the corner of my eye, I watch as Frank takes notice of what's going on. Grabbing the water bottle beside him, he throws it at Vik and Joe. The bottle thunks right at their feet, and they both jump from the startling sound. They both look around to see the person responsible, and when their gaze lands on Frank, he does the hand signal showing *cut it out*. They nod their heads in understanding and straighten their clothes, both having to rearrange themselves to hide their bulging dicks.

Leaning back in the throne, I start to pout that my show was cut short and a brilliant idea pops in my head. Jumping up from my perch, I briskly walk over to Vik and Joe and grab their hands. "Come on, guys, dance with me!" Without giving them a chance to refuse, I drag them down two sets of stairs and straight onto the dance floor. With our luck, a great song was playing so we quickly got lost to the music. Stepping in between them, I become the center of their attention. My hips gyrate in beat with the music, and as the jam slows down to a more sensual one, I begin to grind against both of them. Their tucked-away dicks harden back to their impressive lengths and press against me in the most delicious ways.

Raising my arms, I wrap them around Joe who stands behind me and press against him even harder, earning me a throaty groan. His hands grip my hips as he grinds his length against me, and then Viktor closes the distance between us and slides his hand up my dress finds his way into my drenched pussy. A moan escapes me as he adds another digit and begins to thrust his long fingers, making sure to brush against that soft spot deep inside. Looking up at my two men that have me sandwiched between them, I can only envision the way they were not too long ago. "Kiss him, take his mouth like your finger is taking my pussy!"

With my command, they do as I say and slam their mouths together just above me. Vik's fingers only falter for a second and then he beings to finger-fuck me with the same intensity that he savages Joe's mouth with. His fingers are like the outlet of the desire and passion that is overflowing between them, which makes me climb to the peak and with a swipe of his thumb on my clit, I explode. My channel clenches around his fingers that are still pumping inside of me and my clit throbs underneath his thumb as he continues to swirl it unrelentingly.

Arching my back against Joe, I try to pull off of Vik's hand, but he only presses closer, which allows Vik to push even deeper. Leaning forward, I bury my face in his chest to muffle the moans he is ripping from me. The orgasm I was trying to fight off builds with such intensity, thanks to the alcohol behind it, and only seconds after my first orgasm, I explode again. Behind me, Joe tenses as his dick starts to twitch between us and a groan mixed from both of them sounds.

Without missing a beat to the music, Viktor

withdraws his fingers from my quivering pussy and then slides his drenched fingers into his mouth, sucking both of them clean. Not caring if anyone saw what we did, we continue to dance the night way, jizzed pants and all.

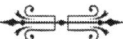

THE REST of the night speeds by courtesy of tequila shots and lots of dancing. After the first couple of songs, Viktor and Joe traded spots with Frank, and as the night went on, they all took turns dancing with me. Of course, during the night, Frank kept making me drink water, which was annoying at the moment, but I know I will appreciate later. After the club closed, I sobered up enough to head to the second floor and help my girls clean up the mess. The time spent with them allowed me to catch up and listen to any of their complaints. Luckily, they all think I'm doing a wonderful job and will support me with whatever I ask of them.

Back on the top floor, I grab another water bottle and point out to my guys. "So who's driving me home? Even with almost an ocean's worth of water in me, I know I'm still drunk."

Viktor hops up as soon as the question leaves me and volunteers. "I got you, babe." Walking over to Godfrey, he whispers something to him, and with Godfrey's nod, they exchange keys, and then he walks over to me. Wrapping his arm around my waist, he leads me toward the stairs.

Looking over my shoulder, I see all three of them grinning as if they know a secret. Shooting a questioning glare at Vik, I start to pry. "What's going on?"

"I don't know what you're talking about, love." Squinting my eyes, I notice the twitch in his cheek like he is fighting back a smile. Damn it, I knew it. He's definitely up to something.

Shaking my head, I decide not to fight it because the energy I got left in me isn't enough to barter with. "Whatever you say, let's just get home and pass out." The rest of the way outside, Viktor doesn't say anything, but he doesn't have to. The damn shit-eating grin on his face yells it for him. As we exit the back doors, I start toward my truck, but Vik pulls me in the opposite direction. Looking at where we are going, I notice Godfrey's matte black motorcycle propped up and ready to go. Whatever lingering effect from the alcohol that I had is now gone. Now wide awake, I stare at the bike with pure excitement.

Viktor slings his leg over the side and straddles the beast between his legs. With the bike balanced between his legs, he starts the bike and pulls the throttle. The roar that comes from the beast makes me so giddy I begin to bounce on my toes. Kicking off my heels, I grasp them in one hand and climb onto the back, making sure to grip Viktor's waist as tight as I can. Once I'm settled, Vik kicks the kickstand up and starts for the road. With it being just after four in the morning, there is no one on the road; so with no mind on the street lights or stop signs, we start to soar down the street.

With the wind destroying my updo, I reach up and toss all the bobby pins out, letting my wavy locks down. My turquoise waves billow out behind me, causing the most freeing feeling ever. Resting my head on Viktor's back, I let the wind blow away the world, leaving only us behind. After what feels like forever, we finally start slowing down.

With my eyes now open, I notice we aren't in the city anymore; instead, we are in the country driving up to a field full of flowers. Stopping at the rickety wooden gate, Vik lowers the kickstand and cuts the engine. After I successfully climb off the bike without busting my ass, I walk over to the fence and use it to balance against as I slide my shoes back on. "What are we doing out here?"

"Trust me, babe, just climb through the fence and come with me. We got to hurry." Listening to Vik's instructions, I duck in between the wooden beams and join him on the other side. Placing my handing in his outstretched one, I stumble as he hustles his way to the top of the hill. With it still dark outside, I nearly trip over a couple of stones and after my last near-fall, Vik scoops me up like a bride and carries me the rest of the way.

With the surprising lift, I start to giggle like a little school girl, but as we reach the top of the hill, I quiet. The scene in front of me is absolutely breathtaking. On the other side of the hill, there is a completely still lake. The crickets and owls have their own orchestra that fills the early morning with a beautiful sound, and the way the moon shines is brighter than I have ever seen before. I nearly tumble out of Viktor's arms so I can stand on my own two feet. Once I'm safely down, I take a couple of steps closer to get a better view. In this field, there is a sparse amount of trees which allows me to get a clear view of the horizon and the slight hue of the rising sun.

After a few minutes, my patient waiting paid off. The sun finally rises, filling the sky with shades of orange and pink. Beautiful arrays of color fill the horizon igniting the day with a burning flame that will fill out the sky with the brightest light. As the glorious sun inches higher in the sky, the fog begins to rise from the lake, causing a haunting effect. I go to reach over to Viktor, but I realize he's not by my side, so I spin around to find him. What I see makes me collapse to my knees right in front of him.

My trembling hands fly to cover my gaping mouth, and the happiest tears start to slide down my cheeks. In front of me, Viktor is kneeling on one knee with a red velvet box that holds a brilliant ruby-encrusted band inside. Clearing his throat, Vik breaks the silence. "Selene, you are the sun to my world, you warm my soul and light up my life in ways I never thought imaginable. I kneel here in front of you with all my love for you fully exposed, so will you, my love, marry me?" With the emotions choking me up, I can only nod my head uncontrollably, and as I continue to nod yes, he grasps my left hand and slides the band onto my ring finger, where it fits perfectly against the ring Frank got me.

Sliding on my knees, I close the distance between us and rasp out, "I love you, Vik, everything about you, so yes, I will marry you."

Twenty-One

"Selene, hurry up! They are going to leave without us!" Octavia's plea for me to hurry makes me smile at myself in the mirror. Little does she know, I'm ready to go, I just can't stop staring at the two shiny rings on my left hand. The glistening rainbow effect is mesmerizing as the jewels' radiance shines onto the walls of my bathroom. With a sigh, I stop admiring the rings and spritz myself with some perfume and exit my bathroom. Tavia, who is laying on my bed, scrolling through social media, looks over to me and rolls off the bed as she sees me ready. "Great! Let's go! I want to have some damn fun before you ship me off."

"You know I'm only asking this of you because I care about you, right? You're my sister, and I gotta protect you." When I first presented Tavia with my wish for her to leave town, she fought like crazy to stay, but once I told her where she would be going, well, let's just say she packed her bags faster than I could finish telling her the details. Apparently, the Bahamas is a place she's always wanted to go.

"Do you see me complaining? I'm okay with a little vacation. I mean, I'm going to miss the shit out of you, but it's not like I'm going to be gone forever."

"This is true, a couple of months max, and while you're there, I'll make sure you are funded, so you're not bored."

Waving me off, Tavia walks out of my room and into the living room where all of my men are huddled. "I'm not worried about it, Selene. I mean seriously, who is going to complain about getting sent to the Bahamas? Not me, that's for sure." Slapping her hands on the back of the couch, she urges the guys to get up. "Come on; we are waiting on you now!" With their heads shaking, they rise from the couches and head toward the front door.

The bar we are heading to is a low-key dive bar that serves all types of liquor along with the best bar food. So each of us is dressed in casual attire, which for me happens to be short jean shorts and a black cami. Octavia is wearing jeans shorts with a shimmery, strapless silver shirt. Thankfully we did because as we walk into the bar, we are blasted with lingering body heat and the heat from the kitchen. Classic rock music blasts from the surround sound speakers and people fill the floor either playing pool or darts or chatting with their friends.

Luckily, we find an open table in the back of the bar large enough to fit us all. We all slide into the booth, except for Frank and Joe, who head to the bar to get our drinks and whatever junk food they are craving. Leaning over, I yell to Tavia, "We are getting on the dance floor tonight, miss thing! So get some of that liquid courage into your system."

"Hell yeah, bitch! We are going to have a fucking amazing night and get so fucked-up we will still be drunk tomorrow!" As she pulls away, she yells out, "Owww owwww!" Her voice is loud enough that the rest of the bar hears her, and then they all begin to mimic her. The vibe in the bar is happy-drunk people excitement—a vibe I can definitely relax in.

Shortly after, Frank and Joe return with their hands full of buckets that are shoved full of bottles and ice. They set the buckets on the table and begin pulling the bottles out and popping their tops, and begin to pass out the beer. With one in everyone's hand, we cheer and clink our bottles together. Some of which sound like they nearly shattered. Just as soon as our cheers are over, we all start to chug our drinks. One by one, we empty our bottles and slam them down with euthanism. With Viktor being the first to finish, he starts popping the tops on our second round and starts handing them out to everyone.

Grabbing my beer, I nudge Tavia and motion for her to slide out. "Let's go play some pool!" Nodding in agreement, she grabs her drink and slides out. Before I can get out of the booth, someone grabs my hand. Looking back, I see it's Godfrey with a questioning gaze. Leaning over, I shout what he wants to know. "We are playing pool; wanna join?" With a shrug of his shoulders, he lets my hand go and begins to slide out after me.

With all the tables full, we linger around and wait for an opening. One of the biker dudes sees us waiting and calls out to us. "You come give me a kiss, pretty lady, and we will let you have this table." The slur in his voice lets us know he has had more than enough to drink, and his behavior is fueled by the alcohol cruising through his system.

Tavia however, doesn't care and plays right along with it. "Oh yeah, *papi*, you just want a kiss, and then we can have the table? I think I can do that for you." The next thing I know, Tavia starts sashaying her way over to the burly, bearded man. She doesn't stop until he is pressed up against the table and her little self is dwarfed by this man. Not batting an eyelash, she runs her pointy nails down the front of his leather vest and whispers something to the beast. Whatever it was, makes him pick her up by the back of her thighs and wrap her legs around his waist. Turning around, he sets her on the table and crashes down on her.

I blink in astonishment that she actually went through with it. Looking over toward Godfrey, I laugh when I see that he has the same expression as I do. Hoots and howls sound around the bar, and when they separate, Tavia lets out another, "Owww owwwwww!" The burly beast lifts her from the table and sets her gently on her feet. As she starts to walk over toward us, he smacks her on the ass hard enough to make her jump and let out a yip. But the way she looks back at him has me losing it.

I start laughing hysterically, and when

Tavia makes it back to my side, she playfully slaps me on my shoulder. "Oh my god, Tavia! You should have seen your face when he slapped your ass!"

"Oh, shut up, you!"

Taking a swig of my beer, I calm my hysterics down and look over to Tavia. "Well, thanks for taking one for the team, now let's go play pool."

"You know, I'll take one for the team anytime if he is involved. That was one of the best kisses I ever had, and that's even with him two sheets to the wind."

"Well shit, go get his number then! You are single bitch; you deserve some good dick!" I watch as a blush creeps up caramel skin and turns her cheeks a rosy pink. He may be a burly biker dude, but if the fucker can treat my main squeeze right, I'm all about supporting her.

As the three of us approach the pool table, the guys currently occupying it hand over their sticks and start to help rack the balls. Once everything is set up, we call order, and then break the balls. Sometime during the middle of the game, the rest of the guys come over with a fresh beer for each of us and watch as we play. The time here at the dive bar is filled with nothing but laughs, jokes, and good memories. Hell, I even win the game of pool, which is a complete shocker to me because I never play.

Deciding to continue to play, we rerack the balls, but this time I go up against Frank and Viktor. With Godfrey not on this round, he goes to the bar and fills our buckets back up. As I wait for my turn to go, Tavia approaches me and talks into my ear so I can hear her without her yelling. "I'm going to the bathroom. It's, um, gonna take a few minutes, so don't go barging in there." When her words register, I lean back and give her a high five.

Pulling her back to me, I say, "You better use a condom! Now go get you some, boo!" She pulls back and lets out a laugh. Shaking her head, she heads in the direction the bathroom leaving me with an approving grin. When Frank looks at me quizzically, I just shake my head and wave for him to shoot, because it's his turn. Rolling his eyes, he gets into position and then lines his cue stick up and shoots for a solid ball. Hitting it true, I follow the ball as it bounces off the side and sinks into the right corner pocket.

Letting out a hoot, he quickly lines up to sink another one. If he gets this one in, there will only be the eight ball left. We all steadily watch as he pulls the stick back, and with a loud crack, he hits the ball. Searing pain shoots through my abdomen, and hot liquid soaks my shirt. Placing my hand on my stomach, I fight not to scream in pain, and when I look down, I realize the reason for my pain. I was shot.

Screams erupt, and more gunfire starts exploding all around me. The pool table that we were just playing on is tossed to its side, and I'm dragged behind it. Frank's frantic face moves in front of me, and I watch as his mouth moves, but nothing comes out. Looking down, I lift my hand and see it covered in my blood. Frank's gaze follows mine, and when he sees the wound, he rips his shirt off and shoves it on the wound. I scream out in pain from the pressure and tears start to run down my face. This wound is nothing like the graze when Neal shot me; this is worse.

It feels like my insides are melting, and my skin is on fire. The blood that is pumping out of me feels like lava as it gushes out of the opening. Wood shards fly off the pool table, and Frank dunks down to avoid the flying bullets. Reaching to his side, he pulls out his weapon and peeks around the side. I can't watch as he tries to defend me; instead, I look around me and take in the dead bodies of innocent men and women caught in the crossfire between a fucking Italian meatball of a man and me.

I can't let anyone else die because of this shit. With all the strength I can muster, I get to my knees and crawl over to where Frank is. I start to reach in his shirt to get his other weapon, but Frank jumps and nearly knocks me down. "What are you doing! Stay down! We got this!" Shaking my head, I glare at him until he yanks out his secondary from his other holster and slams it in my hand.

Gripping the gun, I crawl over the other side of the pool table and look out. I find Godfrey and Joe taking cover behind the metal tables, and as my search continues, I see Viktor and Jaime behind the bar shooting at the people who are dressed in all black with black ski masks. Observing the rest of the people, I notice some of the other patrons have their weapons out and are trying to defend their partners by shooting at the enemies. I try to count how many people are firing at us, but in the midst of me assessing the situation, they spot me peeking around the table and begin to fire in my direction. Falling back, I take cover and hope for some fucking miracle.

Taking a chance, I stick the gun around the corner and aim in the general direction of the people shooting at us. I don't stop until I use every bullet in the slide and when the slide stays locked back, I pull it back in and call over to Frank for another magazine. As he slides me one of his spare mags, I hear a shotgun blast.

With the amount of blood that I've lost so far, it doesn't surprise me that my vision starts to get hazy, and it takes me longer than it should to reload the gun. When I finally hear the click of the magazine locking into place, I cock the gun and peer around the corner. With all the gunshots that have gone off, we actually killed some of the ones shooting at us. I start to raise my gun to fire, but as I aim to fire, an explosion sounds followed by a bright white light that knocks me on my ass.

As the ringing clears from my ears, I hear the reason for the explosion. "GET ON THE GROUND! FBI, GET ON THE GROUND! LOWER YOUR WEAPONS! WE WILL SHOOT!" Peeking around the pool table, I spot Jaime with his hands in the air, one holding his gun, the other holding his badge. Thank fuck for him having backup. I don't think we would have survived this. Not with the lack of weapons.

Surprisingly, more gunshots go off, and in rebuttal, the FBI open fire on the cause. With every shot that rings, I fall weaker and weaker. Unable to hold myself up, I lean against the table and drop the gun. Looking down, I see blood seeping out of the completely soaked shirt and covering my hand. Underneath all the blood, a shimmer catches my eye. My rings, the rings promising a life full of happiness. Their glorious sparkle is now a dull shine because of the coagulated blood coating them.

Frank slides over to me and pulls me into his arms and starts to scream for help. I hear him plead for mercy and call for any god to save me. His grip on me is punishing, as if he is trying to hold my soul down, preventing it from leaving my body. His tears drop down to my cheeks and mix with mine. I want to comfort him and tell him that everything is okay, but no words leave me. Only whimpers from the pain that is tearing through me. Joe's frantic face flashes in front of me, and as I roll my head to the side, I see him screaming out.

I can't hear their beautiful voices anymore, and my body is starting to lose its heat. The only thing keeping me warm is the body heat coming from Joe and Frank. I wince as Frank stands and begins to walk with me in his arms. With each jarring step, more pain radiates through me. I try to brace for each step but I'm finding it impossible to tense my muscles. As he walks, faces pass over me, some being my men and then a scream sounds. Tavia, my best friend, my sister.

Knowing that all my men and my best friend are safe and sound, I feel better. I'm not worried about them being in pain or lying on the cold floor. As I start to relax in Frank's arms, he looks down at me and starts to shake me. I watch his mouth through clouded vision and see him yelling at me to wake up. But I am awake. He starts to walk faster and then the next thing I know, we are outside. The night sky glistens with each twinkling star, and shining down on me is the moon. The other half to the sun, its opposite, also its perfect match. They couldn't last without each other.

Something soft is beneath me, and Frank backs away, I want to reach out and keep him at my side, but I can't move. Instead, a man in a paramedic uniform steps over me. His eyes are full of sorrow and determination, I watch as he yells to someone, and then he begins to check for a sign of life. With every passing second, he begins to fade, going further and further away. Everything is cold, and I feel like I'm suffocating. Unable to force myself, I stop trying to breathe.

Twenty-Two

(Joe's POV)

NO, IT can't be. My princess needs to see the light of day. I haven't had the chance to ask her to marry me yet. The red-diamond band feels like a million pounds in my pocket, and all I want to do is jump in the back of the ambulance and slide it on her delicate finger. But with the paramedics back there performing CPR on her, I know I will only be in the way. She will live. I will get the chance to ask her properly, and then my ring will be able to sit on the other side of Frank's, encircling the diamond in the reddest rubies.

    Moisture runs down my face, and with the back of my hand, I wipe it away. As I pull my hand away, a dark smudge catches my eye. Looking closer, I notice that moisture is blood. Well, shit. Sliding my hand over my buzz cut, I find the cause—a shard of glass, likely from the bottles exploding as they get hit by stray bullets. Shrugging it off, I focus back on the man who is saving the woman who has my heart. I count the number of times he compresses her chest to beat her heart for her, and then the times he forces oxygen into her lungs. Thirty and two, on repeat. One that I hope he never stops. Not unless she can do it on her own.

Everything around me is a blur, and all the sounds mix together into a jumbled mess. The only thing I can focus on is her limp hand that is hanging off the side of the stretcher. However, my view is obstructed by the doors of the ambulance. They are slammed shut by the other paramedic, and as soon as they are closed, they zoom away. Absentmindedly, I step in their direction, but a tug on my arm stops me.

Looking back, I see Viktor yelling at me. Shaking my head to clear the fog, I look back toward him. This time, his words are clear. "Joe, let's go, man, we need to get to the hospital. She's going to be okay."

"You don't know that man; she wasn't moving."

"Yes, I do know! She is so fucking strong, and I know damn well she would never give up so easily. Now come on, we need to go." With a final tug, I follow after him. Needing to be close, I capture his hand as his slides past and interlock our fingers. He squeezes my hand, and we make our way to the idling SUV.

Opening the back door, I notice only Frank and Godfrey inside. "Where's Jaime? He needs to be there for her!"

Frank looks over his shoulder to me and

nods his head in the direction of the bar. "He was inside with the agents last time I saw. I tried to get his attention, but the fucker blew me off."

Jerking back in surprise, I shake my head. "Give me two minutes, let me get him! Selene would be pissed if she knew we left him here." Frank's lips thin, but he nods his head in agreement. With a final squeeze to Vik's hand, I take off toward the bar that is overflowing with FBI, cops, and crime scene investigators.

I only make it to the entrance before I'm stopped by a minuscule-looking man with a badge. "You can't come in here; it's a crime scene."

"I know that, but Jaime is with us, I need to speak to him, please it's urgent." As much as I want to push past this asshole, I know that will only put me behind bars, and I can't do anything for my princess there.

With a glance over his shoulder, he lets out a sigh and moves to the side. "Fine, but be fucking quick and stay out of the way." Nodding in agreement, I push past him and begin scanning for Jaime. But what I see does not remind me of someone who just had their loved one rush off in life-threatening condition. No, Jaime stands with his FBI buddies, laughing.

Without getting in anyone's way, I make my way over toward him. As I approach, one of his buddies spots me and tilts his chin in my direction, causing Jaime to look my way. Acknowledging my presence, he turns back to his friends and tells them to hold on a minute. As he starts closing the distance between us, he crosses his arms and gets his expression to a blank slate. "What's up, Joe?"

"'What's up, Joe?' That's it? Selene just got rushed to the fucking hospital, and you're here laughing it up. Do you even fucking love her like you say? You know what, I don't fucking care. Are you coming with us to the hospital or not?" I'm seething, and it's clearly evident in my tone, and my voice was loud enough for his fucking buddies to hear. They look over our way and cover their laughs with fake coughs.

Leaning forward, Jaime clenches his teeth and whispers, "Look, don't fucking stand there and criticize me for not losing my shit. You don't know what's going on on the inside. I'm dying because I know she might not make it, but I can't fucking leave here and hop in a fucking SUV full of known criminals! I will be there as soon as I can break away from here!"

Shaking my head, I spin on my heel and head toward the exit. As I start making my way through the debris, I hear Jaime curse. The next thing I know, he grabs my arm and stalls me in my tracks, "Look, I'll be there okay? I promise." Yanking my arm out of his grip, I push past the staring agents and hurry over to the waiting SUV.

Pulling open the back door, I slide in and slam it shut. At the click of my seatbelt, we haul ass out of the parking lot. The whole way to the hospital, we don't say a single word. With the amount of anger and adrenaline flying around between us, I know one wrong word will cause an explosion. Instead of telling them what Jaime said, I take an inventory on myself. Besides the shard of glass in my head, I feel fine. However, with each passing streetlight, I notice the blood that is splattered on me and my overall disheveled appearance. But after a quick scan of the rest of the guys, I notice that we all look about the same—tattered and distressed. Survivors of a mass shooting.

"Shit! Did anyone see Tavia? Was she okay?" I can't believe I forgot about that crazy chick. If anything happened to her, I know Selene will flip her shit.

With a grunt, Frank says, "I gave Greg our address and told him to take her home. She didn't have anything wrong with her except for being in a panic attack."

"Who's Greg?" Viktor and I question at the same time. Well, at least I'm not the only one who is lost.

Frank looks in the rearview mirror and flicks his gaze to both of us and raises his brows. "That biker she was hanging all over. He's the owner of the gun range I took Selene to. He's good people."

"Ah, well if you trust him to take care of her that's fine with me. If anything happens, I'm blaming it on you. There's no way I'm going to be the one being yelled at by Selene." Even with the severity of the situation, I can't help but laugh at the thought of Selene going toe to toe with Frank. Her perfect slender self against a bulky bodyguard who takes no shit. The others must have envisioned the same thing as me because they all join me in the laughter.

The humor is cut short when the hospital comes into view. Under the starry night, the hospital signs gleam like a beacon, lighting a path for those in need, and yet, there is a darkness about the building—the idea of death lingering in the corners of each wing, waiting to capture the souls of those too weak to survive. I have to bite my tongue to get out of the dark recesses of my mind. Death isn't going to take Selene, and if he tries, she is going to tell him to fuck off.

With it being nearly midnight, there are plenty of places for us to park so as soon as we come to a stop, we all jump out and power walk to the emergency room. Viktor is the first to enter through the sliding doors and makes his way to the receptionist. The rest of us linger in the lobby, knowing for sure that if all four of us approach asking about Selene, the receptionist would be less inclined to give us information.

I start to bounce on the balls of my feet with anxiety, and not knowing anything is only making my nerves worse. I'm a complete wreck without her by my side. Once Vik turns away from the counter, he waves us over, and we start to follow him down the hall. I have to jog to catch up, but once I'm at his side, I question him. "What she say? Any news?"

Vik darts his eyes to me and then over his shoulder to Godfrey and Frank, both right behind us. "She's in surgery. The receptionist couldn't give me much information, but I told her that I was her fiance and her emergency contact, so once there's news, they will let me know." Dread fills my gut, and I try to grasp on the only hope there is. She's alive. She has to be alive for surgery.

When we make it into the waiting room, we

spot a corner section of chairs and take them. In the front of the waiting room, there is another receptionist; this one, however, has no fucking care in the world. She is leaning back in her chair and playing on her phone. I want to yell at her that our fucking life is in surgery right now, but I know that won't help any. I know that counting the seconds that tick by won't make time fast forward.

Propping my arms on my knees, I lean forward and drop my head. My eyes burn from unshed tears, my head throbs from the piece of glass still stuck in there, and my soul aches. Balling my hands together, I start to squeeze them, using my own flesh as a stress ball. A hand lays over top of mine, and when I look over, I see the same expression that I'm feeling on Godfrey's face. Another hand piles on top of ours, but this one belongs to Frank and right behind his is Viktor's. With our hands together, we support each other, being there for each other in a time of need. A family brought together by Selene.

Completely lost in my mind, I lose track of time. Every time the doors slide open, I look up with the hopes to see Jaime. Inwardly pleading he would keep his word. But he never shows, and I'm honestly not surprised. I want to confront and question him for all his action; leaving for days at a time and for never being there when Selene needs him. I start to question the others on their feelings about the situation, but the sound of someone calling a name halts everything. We all jump up in anticipation. "What was the name?"

The nurse clears her throat and repeats

herself. "Romanov?"

Viktor moves forward, and without hesitation, he asks the question we are all begging to know. "Is she alive?" We all pause as we wait for her to respond, and the way she looks back at us almost makes it seem like she isn't going to answer. But when she does, I hear all of us release the breath we were holding.

"Yes, sir, she's alive."

Afterword

A Cliffhanger *Gasp*

I know guys, I know. I promise there is one more book to this story, and whatever questions you have will be answered. I promise!

Hang in there with me and just enjoy the fact Selene is alive <3

Author Note

HOLY SHIT. I just released another book and I totally can't believe it! Dreams do come true, but they didn't come true without you! I want to thank all my readers for believing in me and cheering me on. All your kind words have pushed me to continue writing this series, hell writing in general.

As I write each book, I learn more about my writing style, and all the little things that need improved. So hopefully the next book will be better than the last!

With that being said, I would love it if you left me a review on Amazon. Tell me what you thought, the things I could improve on, the things you wish to see in the series, or even just a few words in general. All reviews matter and I appreciate them all. They help me grow as a writer and not only help me, but help others who look for reviews to see what to read.

Again, Thank you for taking a chance on me and for reading the Lethal Beauty & Smoking Steel Series!

About the Author

YO.

I'm Darcy Ray & I write books.

I'm an RN-BSN who picks up way too many shifts and gets a thrill from codes. I've been married to my soulmate since February of 2011 & plan to spend forever with him. We have four fur babies named Moe, Molly, Hagrid, and Styx. In my free time, I like playing PC games and reading, or hell annoying my wifeys. I'm a Virgo and my favorite color is grey... Oh, wait, this isnt tinder lmao. Sorry, it's been a long year for me, so to wrap this up, stalk me with all my links, ask me anything in my group, and stay up to date!

Xoxo

Amazon: amazon.com/author/darcyray

Fan Group:
https://www.facebook.com/groups/darcysdarlings

Author Page: https://www.facebook.com/authordray/

Goodreads: https://www.goodreads.com/Darcy_Ray

BookBub: https://www.bookbub.com/profile/darcy-ray

Instagram: https://www.instagram.com/darcy_ray_author/

Twitter: http://twitter.com/AuthorDarcyRay

Tiktok: @DarcyRayAuthor

Also by Darcy

Lethal Beauty & Smoking Steel Series

Mafias Kiss: getbook.at/MafiasKiss
Mafias Embrace: getbook.at/MafiasEmbrace
Mafias Revenge: getbook.at/MafiasRevenge

Novellas

Breaking the Mold:
getbook.at/Breakingthemold
Frosted Ember: getbook.at/FrostedEmber
Poisoned Affliction:
mybook.to/PoisonedAffliction
International Love:
getbook.at/InternationalLove

Also Check Out

Keep Reading!

CHAPTER ONE

The sound of the gavel connecting with the judge's podium has to be the most beautiful sound I've ever heard. With the widest smile, I grab my suitcase full of evidence and nod at the witty grey-haired judge who looks at me with bewilderment and says, "Thank you, your honor, for finally setting me free. Now if you'd excuse me, I have a last name to change." With a wink, I exit the courtroom with an extra pep to my step and the soft chuckle of the judge echoing in the shocked room.

Finally, after five years of insufferable family dinners, a nagging mother-in-law, and an increasingly 'thickening' husband, I am free. No more Mrs. Patterson because, as of thirty seconds ago, I won the case for my divorce and acquired all of his assets. That's what the bastard gets - cheating on me for four years isn't enough, no he also stole the family jewels I inherited and gave them to his mistress. I would have never known about the affair if I hadn't gone to his office. The smug secretary blatantly flashed the jewelry at me and when I questioned her, she laughed and had a blase attitude about the whole confrontation.

Learning of his long-term affair filled me

with rage, of all the time I wasted with him, but then I began to realize - this was my escape. So over the next couple of days, I gathered every email, text, call log, and credit card transaction possible. With all that in hand, I contacted my girlfriend, who happens to be a well-known lawyer, and got her on the case. Like my married name, the rest is history.

Wanting to completely erase him from my life for good, I stop by the receptionist's desk and pay an extra fee to leave with the documentation to change my name. With the freshly printed paper hot in my hands, I strut to my blue Beemer and haul ass to the social security office. It only takes me a few minutes to get to the old-school building and thankfully, there is parking right in front.

Popping down the visor, I give myself a once over, making sure to fluff my thick sandy blonde waves and wipe away any rogue lipstick smudges. Sliding out of my car, I pull my pale pink button up corduroy skirt down. Even with thicker thighs that constantly touch, the skirt always finds a way to ride up, making the brown marble buttons that hold it together, bunch up. It only takes a few wiggles and everything slides back into place… barely. The girls are barely covered up by a lace baby pink bodysuit that has thin straps straddling my shoulders and a neckline that accentuates them more than needed. So, wiggling around is mighty precarious.

Satisfied that I won't catch a charge from my outfit alone, I grab my prized paper and lock up the Beemer. The steady clicking of my heels on the concrete and the lively chirping of the birds draw me into a calm place mentally, but that's quickly shattered when I walk into the Social Security Administration. Skidding to a stop, I gape at the number of people crowding the small waiting room - nearly forty people consisting of teenagers fiddling on their cells, mothers soothing their teething toddlers, and old men with sweaty pits.

Arching a brow, I make my way over to the front desk to receive my queue in line. The old biddy behind the desk is vigorously tapping away at the keyboard with her tongue peeking out of the side of her mouth while she concentrates. Her curls that were probably prim and proper this morning, are poofed out and wild. Not wanting to disturb her obviously serious work, I prop my elbows on the counter and gently smile down at her.

"I'll be with you in just a sec, darling." With a few more taps to her worn keyboard, she exits the documents and gives a satisfied nod. "What can I help you w…" Her spin to face me quickly turns a normal interaction with a typical customer to a shell shocked stuttering mess with me, a woman who flaunts her sexuality to the fullest. Instantly her thinning lips pucker in distaste and her body becomes stiff with unease. "What can I do for you?"

Now usually, I would be snippy and call her out on her snap judgment based upon my appearance, but something about her is making me hesitate. Cocking my head to the side, I take in her secretary-like skirt suit, her oversized pearl earrings, and the three shades too light skin complexion where a ring used to sit. "I get it Ms. ... Jones, you don't like how I dress or my bold makeup and riveting waves of hair, but, I'm willing to bet it's not because you think I'm exposing too much. I bet it's because as a young gal, you lived wildly and became the true trollop of the town but then you met the One. You know, the soldier who just joined Uncle Sam and is going to be sent overseas soon. Not wanting to pass it up, you got hitched and fell into domestic wife status without any complaints. But what they don't know is every now and then, you would line your lipstick a little brighter than normal and the charcoal liner would be just a smidge thicker - which gave you a hint of the old life. Years went by and no one questioned it, but now the One is no longer with you, and you feel robbed of all the fun you coulda had." Pausing, I let my words sink in and watch the range of emotions play out on her very readable face. "Now, Ms. Jones, tell me. Am I wrong?"

Her cheeks flush to the brightest shade of red I think I've ever seen and after a few sputtered words she subtly shakes her head no. After clearing her throat, she looks to me once again and mumbles, "How could you possibly know all that?"

Chuckling, I tap the counter with my freshly done acrylic nails and grab my wallet. "Let me give you a card to a lady who has been helping me. When you call, just say Royal referred you and they will understand, and if anything, maybe we can have lunch sometime to compare notes." Sliding a matte black card out, I grab a pen and scribble my cell on the back. With the front facing upwards, I slide it over to her. Hesitantly, she takes the card and looks it over. I see her eyes reread the front a couple of times and when it clicks she looks at me with wide shiny eyes.

Tucking the card into her coat pocket, she straightens in her seat and peers behind me at the line forming. "What are you here for, ma'am?" This time when she asks, it's with a whole new attitude.

"I'm here to make my divorce official. I need my name changed." With a sweet smile, she nods her head and activates the machine that spits out my number. With the little paper in hand, I saunter over to an empty seat and make myself comfortable. Surprisingly my number is called mighty quick which makes me look suspiciously over to Ms. Jones. Sure enough, she gives me a wink and smiles. I guess being as observant as I am, has its perks.

Made in the USA
Middletown, DE
16 May 2022